T0354368

MISFIT

RODNEY S. CAMPBELL

iUniverse®

MISFIT

This is a work of fiction. All of the characters, names, incidents, organizations, and dialogue
in this novel are either the products of the author's imagination or are used fictitiously.

iUniverse
1663 Liberty Drive
Bloomington, IN 47403
www.iuniverse.com
1-800-Authors (1-800-288-4677)

Because of the dynamic nature of the Internet, any web addresses or links contained in
this book may have changed since publication and may no longer be valid. The views
expressed in this work are solely those of the author and do not necessarily reflect the
views of the publisher, and the publisher hereby disclaims any responsibility for them.

Any people depicted in stock imagery provided by Thinkstock are models,
and such images are being used for illustrative purposes only.
Certain stock imagery © Thinkstock.

ISBN: 978-1-5320-2755-0 (sc)
ISBN: 978-1-5320-2754-3 (e)

Library of Congress Control Number: 2017912337

iUniverse rev. date: 09/19/2017

Title of the movie: Misfit

Movie: Focus on one of the characters from Return To Han's Island.

Content: A mixture of a female RAMBO, WOLVERINE and JAMES BOND, combine into one brave, brawny, cutting, clever, wise ass bold heroine. A mix martial arts action movie that show pass and future events of Misfit. It has been ten years since Misfit travel to Han's Island with her teammates. As a member of the CIA assault team, The Barracudas, Misfit was not always a member of The Barracudas. 20 years before she became a CIA agent, she was a navy seal unknowingly working for the Alumnus. A 6 year old girl from Brooklyn who witness the killing of her parents and older brother. Traveling down a trouble pass as a trouble making criminal. When a navy recruiter adapts the trouble teen girl, she become a deadly fighter and heroine. Years later she will faces the vicious assassins that kill her family and changed her life.

Movie time: 2 hrs and 30 minute

Title, Movie, Storyline and Script writen by Rodney S. Campbell

Rating: R-rated movie, contains strong violence, sex, nudity and language.

Brooklyn, New York, year of 1983, time is 8: 12pm. A family eats dinner at the table in the kitchen. They eat and talk, suddenly lound knots come from the outside of the apartment metal door. The Timeworth family stops talking and Mrs. Timeworth looks at Mr. Timeworth. Mrs. Timeworth has a scare look on her face. Mr. Timeworth gets up from the chair to answer the door. Mrs. Timeworth gets up from her chair and takes the children from the kitchen table. They go into a room in the apartment, the mother has make a small hiding place, she puts the older boy and younger girl in a hiding place with in the apartment.

She tells her children to kept quiet and "don't make a sound no matter what happen to mom and daddy," we will come back to get you." Mrs. Timeworth closes the wall shut as the two children cry, scream and yell out for their parents. Older brother and sister hold each other. Tommy:" Mom said for us to stay quiet and not move, stop crying, iam here, mom and dad will be back for us,..ok Michelle." Michelle: "ok Tommy." Michelle and Tommy stop yelling and crying as they hear their mother walk away. Mr. Timeworth opens the door. A single bullet goes through James Timeworth's head. Lisa Timeworth scream out loud, hearing shots fire. Tommy and Michelle slowly put their heads to the sheet rock wall to listen. Mrs.Timeworth screams, yells, crys and argue with the man that just killed her husband.

Mrs.Timeworth:" Oh god." "what did you do" ! "motherfucker." She pushs the man out of the way to try to help her husband, but man gabs her, pushing her to the floor. Proclus:" I won't let you leave me even if you try girl." "If I can't have you," "then no one can have you. Tommy and Michelle can hear the commotion behind the walls. Proclus rapes and kills Lisa Timeworth as her children listen in horror. Tommy and Michelle move their heads from sheet rock wall, they start to cry silently. The apartment goes silent for 5 minute, without any sounds. Michelle and Tommy stay silent, crying, frighten, but they dare not make any sounds, just as their mother told them. Tommy gets up to open the sheet rock wall, Michelle gabs Tommy. Michelle:"

Mom said to stay here until her and daddy come back, Tommy, no." Michelle speaking to Tommy quietly in the hidden space. Tommy moves from the wall and goes to Michelle, he holds his sister and looks at her. Tommy:" Don't worry sister,"... I will be back." Michelle: "No", no, no" Tommy no," please don't,... ok." Tommy looks at the sheet rock wall to the hidden room, that their mother had build months ago. Tommy looks back at his sister. Tommy: "Ok,sister,stay here,ok." I will come back "I promise."

Michelle: "No." Tommy lets Michelle's arms go and goes to open the sheet rock wall. Tommy opens the wall with caution as he steps out and closes the wall back. Tommy reopens the wall again, telling sister, Tommy: "Stay quiet Michelle." Tommy speaking quietly to Michelle and puts his right finger on her lip. He closes the wall back. Michelle goes to the wall, puts her head to the wall, to listen as her brother walks away. Tommy walks out of the room, he goes through the hallway leading to the living room and kitchen. He sees both his parents lying on the floor, bloodly, dead and lifeless. Tommy goes to run to his dead parent's bodies. Proclus comes from behind Tommy, shooting him in the head, then in the back. Tommy's body fells to the floor. Proclus walks over Tommy's bloodly dead body and puts a third bullet into Tommy's neck. The blood flows out of the three bodies onto the floor, walls and every place in the living room. Proclus and three of his assassin search the apartment for any survivors. Proclus:"Anymore of you,Timeworths in here, come out, come out, anyone there." "I guest not." Little Michelle stays silent until Proclus leaves the apartment. Michelle is awaking by two New York police officers responding to the shooting. Michelle gets up, opens the sheet rock wall, runs out of the hidden room. She is nearly shot by one of police officers who is caught off guard by the little girl. Michelle Timeworth is taken to a adoption agency. 6 families adopt Michelle. Each time she is taken in by a families. Michelle becomes older as the time pass. She gets into trouble over and over again and again, hanging out with street gangs, going to juvenile prisons. Michelle is nick name Misfit by other gang members, people on the streets, in the neighborhoods in which she lives in, and out of by the good side of the authorities. Michelle is taken in by the 6 family. A single woman named Mary Rollen. A U.S navy recruiter and a staff sergeant. She rise Michelle as she was rise, with total respect, discipline and total trust, but if someone betray your trust, your respect, then respect and trust means nothing. Mary kepts Michelle out of trouble. Teaches her to do right and helps her to stay in school. Mary: "You are doing great, my little Misfit. "Michelle graduate from high school and goes into the U.S navy. While completing a mission in the U.S navy, Michelle receive a terrible message from the naval base office. Mary Rollen has been killed in a car crash. With Mary gone, Michelle is let alone. She decide to stay in the U.S navy. Michelle serves more years in the U.S navy. She become a navy seal. Michelle Timeworth retakes the nick name ("MISFIT ").

1

The year is 2016, Colonel Bender is in his office, at a meeting, talking on the phone to his superior officers (The Alurnnus). Colonel Bender: "Yes everything is set, yes ma'am,... "yes sir. Superior officers: "Very well, lets hope these are the soldiers we are looking for?" "All the battalions we trained and send have fail, horribly, ...Colonel. "Colonel Bender: "Oh, this time I am sure, they are the ones,...she is the one that will lead them into victory against this .. threat. "Superior officer: "Ok,... remember we can't afford to lose Colonel Bender." Colonel Bender: "Yes ma'am, yes sir." Superior officers:" We trust you know what to do, ...Colonel." Colonel Bender:"Yes ma'am." Superior officers hangs up phones. Colonel Bender:"Oh yes, she's the one, she most denfinitely is the one, get ready to go to hell sun of bitchs." (Laughter coming from Colonel Bender.) Meanwhile, on going training at a remote U.S naval base. Year is 2017, Michelle, now known as Misfit: "See.... you talk too much shit, lady, who is known as Lady Commando: "Watch your head miss crazy ass." Misfit does one of her many tricks and manages to over come the obstacles just as she did with the other obstacle courses before. Everyone on this elite navy seal unit has pass yet other obstacle course. Misfit: "Was that all, is that all you motherfuckers got." Misfit yells out. Misfit: "You gota be kidding me," "right,...someone tell me this is a joke,... right." No this shit can't be real." The whole team suddenly stands at attention. Everyone except for Misfit, who is still talking. She now stands at attention. Colonel Bender: "Ten hun, attention,...that means you too second lieutenant Timeworth." Misfit: "Yes sir. Colonel sir." Colonel Bender:"Very good, you finally decided to shut your fucking mouth Timeworth, at easy seal team." "My name is Colonel Steven Bender of the U.S pentagon strategic forces." "Now listen up,.. you sorry asses, you miserable sea bitchs." "Today,..one or more of you will be chosen for a very special mission, understand." The whole platoon reply: "Yes sir, Colonel sir." Misfit: "Sir," "can I ask what makes this mission so special from any other mission we have been send on, sir." Colonel Bender: "You will find out soon enough Timeworth. You happen to be one of the candidate chosen for this special mission." Everyone stands back in attention. Colonel Bender tells the platoon to stand at attention and prepare to fall out. The whole platoon reply: "Yes sir, Colonel sir." Colonel Bender: "Fall out." Platoon dismissed." The whole platoon: "Yes sir, sir.! Colonel Bender: "Second lieutenant Timeworth, come with me. "Misfit: "Yes sir." Colonel Bender: "The rest of you return back to your barrack." The rest of the platoon reply: "Yes sir. Colonel sir.! Colonel Bender: "Follow me Timeworth."

Misfit: "Yes sir, right behind you Colonel." Colonel Bender leads Misfit to his office on the naval base. Colonel Bender: "Have a seat Timeworth." Misfit: "So sir,.. whats this about.?" Colonel Bender: "I have been watching you in action, growing stronger, training harder, leaning faster, becoming one of our finest sailors and navy seals." You are dam tough with a capital T." "That's a real great accomplishment, considering what you have gone through." Misfit: "Thank you sir. "Colonel Bender: "You are here because I know you can accomplish even more greater challenges." Misfit: "What did you have in mind Colonel. "Colonel Bender: "Let me show you second lieutenant." The Colonel shows and reads to Misfit about the training. Colonel Bender: "You will receive a higher rank, and all the perks that come with that rank." " Sounds good, second lieutenant." "Misfit: "Ok Colonel, go on." The Colonel continues to show and tells Misfit about the plan to enhance her training as a navy seal. Colonel bender: "Does this sound interesting to you, second lieutenant, or am I boring you.?" Misfit: "Yes, I could use the extra cash." The training sound hard, but for me, it will be easier then a seal in water. Colonel Bender: "So, can I count on you, second lieutenant to be even better.?" Misfit: "Yes sir, when can I get started Colonel.?" Colonel

Colonel Bender: "I like your enthusiasm, second lieutenant." "In two days be ready to ship out, second lieutenant Timeworth. Misfit: "Yes sir Colonel sir.!" Colonel Bender: "See you in two days, second lieutenant." "Are there any more questions or anything else you would need Timeworth.?" Misfit: "Oh yes,… that new rank is already mines sir." Colonel Bender: "Let see second lieutenant Timeworth,… we shall see." "You can go now Timeworth." Misfit: "Yes sir.!" Lady Commando: "So,… what happen,… how did it go, tough girl, tell me what happen between you and the Colonel." Misfit: "Ok, would you relax Lady." Lady Commando: "No, tell me, what happen and then will relax. Misfit: "I have been chosen for the special mission." "I will get higher pay, more benfits and get this,… when I pass all my test,…then I receive the rank of captain." Which means,… more pay vacations, time off." Lady Commando: "That's great tough girl,…well are you prepare for this."

Misfit: "Lady,…do killer whale kick ass." Lady Commando: "Alright then,..you should be fine." "Kick ass tough girl." For two days Misfit and Lady Commando prepare themselves extremely hard for the tests and special missions. The end of the second day comes. Misfit and Lady Commando gear up body and mind. Lady Commando: "Are you really ready for this.?" Misfit: "Yes,…I was born for this." Lady Commando: "Yea, I wish I was coming with you tough girl." Misfit: "Hey, probably I can speak to the Colonel and see what he can do.?" Lady Commando: "Really,…no shitting, your joking with me, right, tough girl." "Misfit: "No shitting and no joking around, bet,….I will call the Colonel now." The next morning comes and Both women are up at the first sign of dawn. Misfit: "Ready Lady."

2

Lady Commando: "No tough girl,… the question is,… are they ready for us." Misfit, Lady Commando and the other navy seals stand at attention in the navel training field. Colonel Bender: "Stay as you are people." Misfit, Lady Commando and their unit continue to stand at attention as Colonel Bender speaks. Colonel Bender: "Second lieutenant Timeworth lets go, you, I and the other candidates have a long trip ahead us." Misfit: "Yes sir, sir before we go,. ..did you consider what we discuss." Misfit: "So,…can second lieutenant Headman come with us on the missions.?" Colonel Bender: "No she can't come, Timeworth this is the navy, not dam high school." Now, does anyone eles have any friends, they would to invite on our missions." "Seals, you are being trained for a special mission." "You are not taking a math test for Ms.Handover." "Last and lease, but just as important, I am a Colonel in one of the worlds largest, greatest and finest navy." I am not a school teacher in a class room." "No, second lieutenant Headman, you can not come on the missions. Lady Commando: "Dam sir, Can't you at lease try to make an exception sir." Colonel Bender: "I don't think you hear me Headman,...the answer is no, now get your ass out of my sight." Lady Commando: "I understand sir." Colonel Bender: "Very good Headman,…now,!" everyone prepare to fall out and report for duty." "Second lieutenant Timeworth come with me, please." Misfit: "Colonel sir, can I say good bye to Headman." Colonel

Bender: "Why, yes,but make it short and sweet, Timeworth, see you out side in five minute,... remember,..five minute, second lieutenant." Misfit: "Yes sir." Misfit and Nina hug each other. Misfit: "Well,...this is it lady, lady commando: "I can't believe this is it." Misfit: "Remember,...short and sweet, fucking Colonel." "I only have five minute,...oh three minute." Lady Commando: "listen, you take care of yourself, kept those dukes up, stay on your toes, fight hard and win harder." "Ok tough girl." Misfit: "Take care of my unit, look after the platoon, your in charge now." "This is not good bye lady and not the end, not by a long shot, only a transfer in plans." "Love you sister, well,... gota go."Lady Commando: "No, this is not good bye." "Give me a big hug tough girl,make it count for something." "love you sister." The other members of the unit give salutes, hugs and kisses good byes to Misfit. Misfit: "look after the second lieutenant you guys." "Second lieutenant Headman, your in charge of the platoon unilt I get back, see you later people." Misfit leave her platoon in the hands of Lady Commando and returns back to Colonel Bender. Misfit: "Ready sir." Colonel Bender: "Ok, lets do this ladies and gentleman." Misfit: "I am Ready for anything and everything, ha, let's do this." Misfit and the other navy seals go into the black military vans. The vans start up, following the navy mp cars and humvees in front the convoy. Colonel Bender: "Move out corporal."Corporal: "Yes sir." Colonel Bender: "Yes madam, yes sir, fades one is completed." Colonel Bender: "Good bye." The callers at the other end of the phone lines hang up."(The Alumnus). The vans, cars and humvees move rapidly down the navel base roads. Going on to the navel highway leading to the navel airport and hangers. Misfit and the other navy seals look out the van's windows as the navel base scenery changes. The memory of her conrad,Lady Commando pops into her head every now and then.

The Colonel gives orders to the military convoy. Colonel Bender: "Ok people, lets move it, move it, move it, everyone on your best." "Your test starts now." The convoy quickly gets to the navel airport. Misfit and the other navy seals move fast, getting on board the military planes. The Colonel follows right behind them. The planes doors come up and close completely as the Colonel gives the order to take off to the pilots. He sits next to the pilots in the cockpit, watching Misfit. He tells the navy seals and Misfit to lock themselves in their seats as the planes move down the runway. The planes move faster and faster down the runway. Pilots: "This is your captain james Dickson, clear for take off, tower. "U.S navy personal in the air, tower: "You are clear for take off captain." Pilots: "Thank you tower." The planes take off, one after the other, going into the air like birds of prey. The Colonel, Misfit and the other navy seals take out some chewing gum and start chewing. The planes fly for 7 and half hours, then, Colonel Bender unlocks his seat belt. Colonel Bender: "All right people, it's time to put on your parachutes, the parachutes are locate up and behind you." The Colonel shows Misfit and the other navy seals the parachutes. Colonel Bender: "Lets move quickly, we only have a few minute." The planes's door open slowly and stop at a standing position. Misfit and the other navy seals give the Colonel a loud, "yes sir, as they put their parachutes on. Misfit and the other navy seals give the Colonel a, "we are ready sir." Colonel Bender: "Very good people." Ok,…here we go." All the planes doors open. Only skies, clouds in the distance and some land can be seen. Colonel Bender: "Jump.!" Misfit: "With pleasure sir.!" Misfit jump out of the plane. Colonel Bender: "Next.!" The Colonel continues to tells the navy seals to jump out the planes, until he jump out of the plane. The captain of the plane, closes the plane's door after getting the signal from private first class blackwater to close down the plane's door. The other plane's crew do the same. They dispatch the navy seals from the other planes. Captain: "Have a nice trip and good hunting navy seal." Good luck Colonel." Misfit enjoys the wind as she and the other navy seals, and Colonel Bender parachutes closer to their location. As the navy seals get closer to the ground, they quickly open their parachutes and began to land onto the ground. Misfit and Colonel Bender are closer than the others. Colonel Bender: "Stop playing those dam games,…young lady.!" Misfit flows on the air, gliding up and down, down and up, up, up in the air, getting even closer to the ground. Colonel Bender: "Open your parachute,… you fucking… Misfit: "Soon sir.!" Colonel Bender: "There's no more room,,…open your fucking parachute,…dam it, now,…second lieutenant.!" Colonel Bender: "Open it,..now.!" "Your,… going to fuck up the mission.!" Colonel Bender seeing the ground come closer and closer, opens his parachute. He lands hard to the ground. Misfit: "Open your parachute sir.!" Laugh ("ha,ha,ha.!") Misfit opens her parachutes, leaving her 15 feet from the ground.

Misfit: "yes,..."we are coming in for a hard landing, just the way like it,"Wow." Misfit lands very hard. Just the way she like it. Misfit: "Wow, Wof, Wof," laughing ("ha,ha,ha.!") Misfit pulls off the parachute and goes to joins the Colonel and the other navy seals. Misfit squat with the other navy seals in a hiden location. The Colonel and the other navy seals look at Misfit with surprise. Misfit: "Surprise.!" Colonel Bender: "Are, you fucking crazy, you could have killed the mission with your stunt." Timeworth, are you some type of nutcase." Everyone looks out onto the island, sandy, grassy, jungle like territory. Colonel Bender: "Timeworth, I asked you a question,...are you crazy." "Timeworth." Misfit: "Yes, yes sir, I am very crazy." "A psycho, maniac nutcase, sir." Colonel Bender: "Follow my orders, you understand me." Misfit: "Copy that sir." Colonel Bender: "Everyone move out and follow me." Misfit and the other navy seals: "Yes sir," Colonel sir." Misfit and the other seals follow the Colonel. Some of the navy seals talk about Misfit being a nutcase. Navy seals: "She should have being dead. Misfit: "Little punk ass pussies." The Colonel gives Misfit and the other navy seals the order to stop." Colonel Bender: "We are here." Misfit, the other navy seals don't know what the Colonel is talking about. Misfit:" Excuse me sir,..here where.?" As the other navy seals look around, they ask the same question. Where are they. Colonel Bender: "Look directly in front of you."

Suddenly, looking very carely and with the Colonel pointing to the hiden fortress to Misfit and the other navy seals. Colonel Bender: "Lets move it." Come on, rapido, vamos, move it." Misfit and other navy seals quickly move behind the Colonel. Following Colonel Bender into the fortress. The Colonel, Misfit and the other seals disappear into the fortress. Misfit, the other navy seals look around the fortress just like kids on a camping adventure. Misfit, thinking to herself, "wow." Some fucking setup you got Colonel." The other navy seals find the hiden fortress very impressly as well. Colonel Bender: "Yes,you like it,… I take it, very good, because you all will be training here as of tomorrow moming, 5:00 am, follow me people, let me show you around. The Colonel show Misfit and the other navy seals around the hiden fortress. The Colonel shows them every part, everything in, and on the fortress. Colonel Bender: "Now that I have shown you your base of operation. The Captain will show you to your sleeping quarters.

Get some r and r. Misfit and the other navy seals give a yes sir, Colonel sir." The other navy seals reply: "Good night sir." The Captain takes over and tells Misfit, the other navy seals to stand at easy. The Captain calls name from his writing pad. Captain Stanly: "Second lieutenant Timeworth." Misfit: "Yes sir," Captain sir." Captain Stanly: "Second lieutenant,...your sleeping quarter are in apartment-A of section-B2."

Misfit: "Thank you Captain sir." Captain Stanly: "Fall out second lieutenant Timeworth, good night." Misfit: "Yes Captain sir," good night." The Captain gets his writing pad out again and goes down the line of navy seals by their ranks. Each navy seal is given a sleeping location based on their ranks. Misfit and one of the other recruit share a sleeping quarters. Misfit: "It looks like you and I are going to be sleeping together. Second lieutenant Peal Dolon: "Hey, that fine with me." Both women start laughing out lound. Misfit: "Second lieutenant Timeworth." Everyone that know me, call me tough girl." Second lieutenant Peal Dolon: "Second lieutenant Peal Dolon, nice to meet you, come here offen, tough girl, you can call me Peal. Misfit: "I will take this bed here. Peal: "And, I will take this bed here, good night." Misfit: "Sleep tight, don't let the bed bug bite." Both women start laughing out lound and go to bed. Dawn breaks, revealing the morning sky. Colonel Bender: "Attention everyone, wake up,! wake up.!" Captain Stanly: "Time to get up." Misfit: "l am,...up sir." Peal: "So l am I sir." Misfit: "See,... we are up sir." Misfit and the other navy seals meet in the training camp with in the fortress. Colonel Bender: "Today people,... we will retraining to do the impossible,.. until the training and the mission is completed, understand people." Misfit and the other navy seal reply: "Yes sir." Colonel Bender: "Now I will leave you in the capable command of Captain

Stanly." Captain Stanly: "Listen up people." "As of now, your asses belong to me, this training will test your mental and physical conditioning." Does everyone understand this." All the navy seals reply: "Yes sir,!" except for Misfit. Misfit: "No sir," I don't understand you." Captain Stanly: "What was that second lieutenant Timeworth." Misfit: "I said,.. I didn't understand." Captain Stanly: "I hear you the first time Timeworth." What is it, you don't understand Second Lieutenant." Misfit: "I am mentally challenge, sir." Captain Stanly: "Alright," Second lieutenant,...I will be the jugde of that." Misfit and the other navy seals go through the hardest, roughest, toughest, mental and physical training. Training that requires Misfit and the other navy seals to pass their physical and mental tests. Each day of training and testing become harder and harder, and harder. Some of navy seals can't take on anymore training and drop out. Those that do not pass are immediately sent back to their bases. Misfit: "Yea, yea, bring it, that right, that it, bring on more shit, bring it motherfuckers, come on." Misfit and just a few other navy seals pass their mental and physical training, and testing on that next day. The training and testing go on for sereral days. Weeks that turn into months. Misfit with only seconds to go. Misfit: "got it, got dam- it, who's the woman," who's the woman." The woman is me, got- dam -it," me." Captain Stanly: "Calm down second lieutenant, stop showing off." Your getting cocky Timeworth."

Misfit: "sir. "I was not showing off." "I have nature skills, sir." Captain Stanly shakes his head up and down. The Colonel looking from a hiden camera, watching Misfit's every move. She completes one test after the other test. As the test become harder, she become even harder. The Colonel shakes his head up and down. Colonel Bender and Captain Stanly write down everything they see Misfit do in their reports. Watching how all the navy seals are doing. Misfit is at the top of the list for the mission that is ahead. Misfit and the other small teams of navy seals get closer to finshing their tests. Soon units, platoons and battalions are formed from all branches of the world's military. The test go on, even more candidates drop out. Only Misfit, a small battalion of navy seals and a football size battalion of global military special forces, are standing in front of the Colonel and Captain Stanly. After weeks of hardcore training, only the best of the best are left. The tests continue, testing every mental and physical being of Misfit and the other combatants. Still more testing and training is given. Misfit and the others get even harder, becoming smarter, passing each test. Captain Stanly: "Very good people, you have passed every test and completed all your training with flying colors." "Good job people, you should be very proud of yourselfs." Misfit and the other combatants reply: "Thank you sir.!" Misfit: "Uh,...isn't there more." Captain Stanly: "What, you want more Timeworth."

Misfit: "Are there more tests." Ahhhh,!" I want more." Misfit talking out lound. She can not be silent or tone down by anyone or anything. Captain Stanly: "With those words said, here is the Colonel."Ten hut, attention.!" Colonel Bender: "Stand as you are, relax people, for you have one more big test to pass" The Colonel and Captain Stanly looking at Misfit more than the others. Colonel Bender: "Fortunately,..for all of you, this training couses will be short and to the point." "The next and last test, will test all your mental and physical strengths.

Misfit: "Yes,.. real good." Great." I love it already." Colonel Bender: "What, was that Second lieutenant Timeworth." Misfit: "Oh nothing sir." "I was just a little excited, sir." The Colonel continues to speak to Misfit and the other combatants. Misfit, listen with great excitement. It is the next morning. All around the fortress the alarms ring to wake up the troops. Misfit: "Good morning." Peal: "What, what." Misfit reads the papers and does some push up. Peal: "Your up," wow." Misfit: Yes, you didn't hear the alarms, lound as hell." "I said good morning Peal." Peal: "Oh,..Good morning." "From the sounds of things,....it time to get up anyway." Misfit: "Yea morning." Misfit: "Time to get up sleepy head." Peal: "What time is it." Misfit: "It just tum to 3 :50am. Peal: "Why are they sounding the alarms so early." Misfit: "I have no ideal." Won't you go find out." Peal: "You Doing something special, how long have you been up." Misfit: "First,..Iam not doing anything special,...and second,...I have been up since 2:50am." Peal: "Doing what,... if you don't mind me asking." Misfit: "Reading and doing my push-up, if you don't mind." Peal: "Actuality,....do you mind if I join you.?"

7

Misfit: "Come, don't get in the way, thou, ok." Peal: "Ok,..cool, tough girl." Mistit: "And kept up, alright." Misfit continues to do push-ups and reads the papers on the floor. She is now joined by Peal. Peal: "Yea, oh, yea ok." Misfit looks at Peal, they read and do push-ups until they hear a lound knot on the door. The Captain opens the door, entering the barrack. Captain Stanly: "Hey,… you ladies up." Misfit and Peal stand at attention. Misfit and Peal reply: "Yes sir." Captain Stanly: "Good,..real good ladies, you can continue on, always be ready, carry on." Misfit and Peal reply: "Yes sir." Misfit and Peal continue to read and work out, until it's time to go pass the last test. The time is now 6:00am. Misfit and Peal are ready. Captain Stanly: "Time to get up ladies." "Oh, you girls still up, lets go ladies." Misfit: "Yes sir," Captain sir." Peal: "Yes sir," Captain sir." Misfit, Peal and the other combatants make up two affective battalions of fearless fighters. The two battalions will soon join up with a extremely, enormous fighting force. The two battalions stand at attention and battle ready. The Colonel and the Captain stand in front of the two battalions. Colonel Bender: "Good morning people." Misfit, Peal and the other combatants reply: "Good morning sir." Colonel Bender: "Today, is the last of the testing. "The Captain will say a few words before the last test." Captain Stanly: "Today I will be showing you the last test." All of you must pass this test,..that's if you are so luck to pass." "I hold a rank for each of you who make it through this test." Good luck, people." Captain Stanly: "Thank you Colonel sir." Misfit, Peal and the other combatants reply: "Good morning sir." Captain Stanly: "Today,...the last test will be a simulation of the mission you have all been training for." Follow me everyone." Captain Stanly takes Misfit, Peal and the others to the simulated test sight. Captain Stanly: "This test will determine if you are the right person to take on and complete this mission. "Colonel Bender: "Captain Stanly start the test." Captain Stanly: "Yes sir." Ten-hut people, the test will began in five minute." Misfit, Peal and the others reply: "Yes sir." Misfit, Peal and the other combatants get ready for the simulated test. Captain Stanly: "Listen up people." In one minute, that red light will tum green,...to signal that you will engage the enemies in the simulated war." Get ready for action, people.!" Misfit, Peal and the other combatants get ready for action. Everyone puts their safe switch to off on their riles and pistols. Misfit: "It's about time, let go Peal." Peal: "Right tough girl." Misfit: "You cover my ass, and I will cover yours."

"Understand Peal." Peal: "Understood tough girl." "I got your back, partner." Misfit: "And I got yours, partner." Misfit, Peal and the other combatants stand prepared to do battle with the enemies in the simulation. Misfit: "Try to stay alive guys." "Stay on your toes,….there are foot prints, shit, they are here." The last test has began without them even knowing. One of the combatants reply: "Where." The other combatant reply: "Where are they." Misfit: "Kept quiet and take cover," you guys are forgetting all your training." "Stop letting your fears take control." Remember what you were trained for." Misfit talking quietly to the other combatants. Misfit: "Take cover." The other combatant reply: "Do you see them." One of the combatants saids this silently to Misfit. The other combatant reply: "Oh shit, shit,…where are they." Misfit: "The bastards are all around us." Suddenly, rapid gun fire comes from all directions. Misfit: "Everyone stay down." Peal: "Everyone calm down and stay quiet." Misfit: "Any of you get up and your are dead." Just then, one of combatants stands up and starts firing his rile in all directions. Combatant (1): "Come on you fucking bastard." Come on." Combatant (1) is killed by one bullet to the head, other bullet goes into her left leg, and the other bullet to her stomach. Finally, the last bullet to her chest. Some of the combatants start to scramble, as combatant (1) falls dead to the ground. Combatant (1) is taken out of the simulation and is brought back to reality. Peal: "This game is so fucking real." "Oh shit, kept your dam heads and asses down." "What do we do next tough girl." Misfit: "Must be some type of trick, a mind game or something." Peal: "Toughgirl,....toughgirl." Misfit: "Wait, wait, Iam thinking." "Stay down and create a full circle." "Laid down gun fire in the directions of the flashing green lights." Combatant (2) stands up. She is shot in the face. Misfit takes a count of the two combatants pulled out of the simulation. The two combatants are escorted out of the simulation. Misfit talking to herself for a monument. Misfit: "they are not really dead, because it's a simulation. Misfit, Peal and the five other combatants return fire. Firing their weapons in all direction of the enemy. Misfit can now see some movement. Misfit tells the others to "stay in place and stay down." "Stay calm and continue to return fire at the moving shadows. Peal tells the other combatants in the platoon to stay down, and in place. Peal: "Stay here, stay down and continue to laid down gun fire." Misfit continue to move in the direction of the enemy and fires at the moving figures in the woods. Bombs and grenades explode into mist of fragments, fire and smoke. The enemy begins to panic, as they run out of hiding spots. Misfit can see more enemy soldiers coming into her range of fire. Enemy soldiers die, as Misfit, Peal and the other combatants fire opon them. Misfit: "Cover me partner." Peal: "You got it partner." Misfit gets down on her neels. She gets up very quickly,moving in the direction of the dead enemy bodies. The death count continue to go up on both sides. Misfit sees the dead enemy bodies disappear. Misfit: "Iam going to beat this game." Misfit continues to fire her weapon. She kills more enemy soldiers. She runs out of bullets, reloading her m 16 single grenade launch rile. Misfit comes out of no where on top of the enemy nest.

Misfit continues to shoot bullets and throw grenades at the enemy. She has killed and injured many enemy soldiers in the simulated combat test. She continues to fire opon the enemy, untll all the enemies in the nest are killed. Misfit speaks to peal on a two-way walkie-talkie. Misfit: "This is Second lieutenant Timeworth, Iam in the enemy's setup." "Everyone is dead on this side. Misfit: "l repeat, Iam in the enemies setup, I killed everyone." Peal: "I hear you, copy that, Timeworth." "We are here partner, I repeat, we hear you, copy." "Listen, we could use some of that brains and bronzes on this side. Misfit: "Listen, kept firing on those asshole, copy." Peal: "Right, copy,...kept firing guys." Misfit finds a way to come from behind some of the enemy units in the other nest. Misfit: "Peal, continue to laid down more fire power on them. Peal: "Got you, time to stay low to the ground guys, come on, lets move out and continue to kept firing." "Kept moving towards the direction of the enemy's nest. Combatant (3): "Are you sure lieutenant." Peal: "Yes, Iam very sure, move, lets move people." Peal and the other combatants continue to move quickly towards the enemy nests. Misfit, Peal and the other combatants kill or injure the simulated enemies. Captain Stanly: "Very good,...time to move on to next level of the test." This time the red lights changes to go green immediately. Rifle and pistol fire come down opon Misfit, Peal and the other combatants. Misfit: "Everyone find some cover,…now" Misfit, Peal and the other combatants run for cover, as they are fired opon. Misfit, Peal, the other combatants find cover behind large objects in the simulated battlefield. Peal: "You ok partner." Misfit: "No, I won't be ok,…until I kill all those fuckers." Peal, Misfit and the other combatants throw, and launch grenades. Misfit gives the signal to everyone in her platoon to charge the enemy. Peal, Misfit and the other combatants continue to engage the simulated enemy soldiers. The enemy soldiers continue to come rushing out from their hiden places, while the grenades go off. Misfit, Peal and the others take out fleaning enemy troops.The other combatants continue to take cover and laid down fire power on the enemy troops. Misfit, Peal and some of the others come out from cover. They kept firing their weapons at the enemy soldiers. The enemy soldiers continue to run out of their hiding places. The enemy soldiers meet with a rain of bullets and grenades. Misfit, Peal and the other combatants stand up and start running and yelling out orders. They continue firing their weapons at the distorted enemy. Misfit tells Peal to drop to the ground. Misfit: "Kept firing Peal." Peal: "Got it." Misfit tells and signals to the other combatants to continue to laid down some major fire power. Misfit, Peal and the other combatants fire their weapons at the on coming simulated enemy troops. Firing bullets, firing rockets, firing grenades from their rifles and pistols.

10

Misfit, Peal and the other combatants throw grenades at the simulated enemy troops. They make their own cloud of smoke from bullets, grenades and bombs launched at the enemy. Misfit and Peal continue to cut down and go through enemy troops. Mean while, the other combatants in their platoon fire every bullet, rocket, grenade and every other projectile from their arsenal into the enemies stronghold. Misfit gives Peal and the other combatant troops in her platoon continuous orders to laid down gun fire. They continue to fire their weapons, killing more enemy troops. The second group of enemy troops are killed. Captain Stanly: "Ready guys, that was good, real good,... good team work people, get ready. "The lights go from red to green quickly. One of the combatants (4) reacts too quickly, by running into the kill spot. Combatant (4) is killed by a cross fire of bullets. Misfit: "Everyone stay down, and take cover," dam, shit, motherfucker." Peal: "Now there are only 15 of us," we are running out of people." Misfit: "Relax, relax." In front of Misfit, Peal and the others, stands a very large black camouflage brick building. Peal: "I have a idea." Misfit and the others move in closer, listen to Peal. Peal speaks to what is left of their platoon. Mean while, Misfit continues to fire her weapons at the enemy troops coming out, and in front of the house. Peal: "Ok, I and Timeworth will act like two surrendering soldiers, right tough girl. "Misfit: "Right. "Peal: "We will detract the enemy, while you three take sniper spots." "Soon as the time looks right, you guys know what to do." The three combatant snipers (5)-(6) (7): "Yes ma'am, we got you sister, we got your backs, Dolan and Timeworth," you got it guys," you can count on us." Misfit: "That your only plan." Peal: "No, when I give you guys the signal to move in, you attack. You come from the back and you come from the front." "You follow behind us." The combatant snipers reply: "Yes ma'am." Misfit: "Ok,...I can go with that." Misfit and Peal fix their selfs up to look injured. Hoping the enemy soldiers will not shoot them and fall into their trap. Misfit: "Allright, ready." Peal: "Sure as ready as any other bad ass. Misfit: "Lets get the rest of those punk assess." Peal and Misfit come out of the dusk, smoke and weapon smoke clouds. The two women look very injured, confused and unarmed. The two women are ready to surrender, carrying a white flag. High ranking enemy soldiers surround by other troops. high ranking soldiers: "A white flag,...they have given up," tell the others we have won." Misfit and Peal yell out, "we give up, please don't shoot, don't shoot, don't shoot, we surrender." The high ranking enemy officers tell the other soldiers to prepare for victory. High ranking enemy officer: "Good, they had a change of heart,...and a change of mind, you bitchies had enough." Wait until they come in the building with us,...then, torture them, rape them and kill them both, understand." Enemy soldiers: "Yes madam." The high ranking enemy officer in charge of the small enemy battalion has no mercy for capture enemies. High ranking enemy officer: "Come on, we won't shoot you, don't shoot them, that's it, come here."

"Everyone hold your fire, we will not hurt you." Misfit: "We give up, we can't take it any more." Peal: "We give up, please, don't shoot us." High ranking enemy officer: "Go get them and be care." Misfit: "We give up, no more fighting,...you win." Misfit speaks silently to the three combatant sniper by her hiden walkie-talkie. Misfit: "Look, we are right here." Meanwhile, the three snipers listen in closely. They prepare to fire at the enemy troops surrounding Misfit and Peal. Misfit: "Come on and get some." Peal speaking in silent with Misfit. Peal: "Yea come." The greeting party of enemy soldiers walk Misfit and Peal towards the large, black, camouflage, brick building. Suddenly one of the enemy soldier turns to see what is behind him. A bullet to the head kills him instantly. Misfit and Peal drop to the ground. A rain of bullets, grenades and rockets hit, kill and injure enemy soldiers. Misfit and Peal quickly pick up weapons from dead enemy troops. The two women start firing at the enemy soldiers and high ranking enemy officers. The high ranking female enemy officer take cover with some of the other enemy troops. The enemy troops and high ranking enemy officer fire their weapons back at Misfit, Peal and their platoon. Misfit, Peal and the other combatants kill all the high ranking enemy officers, except for the one enemy female officer. Enemy troops fire bullets and throw grenades. Misfit and Peal take off running for cover. Misfit: "Shit, that sure didn't work, but it was fun." Combatant (5) Scorpion: "What just happen." Peal: "I guest they don't like the taste of bullets." Misfit: "I guest not, ha, ha, ha." "Time to do things my way,...the hard way." The enemy troops fire continuously at Misfit, Peal and their platoon. Round after round of bullets miss Misfit and Peal. Some of the combatants in their platoon are not so luck. Misfit and Peal continue to retreat to, what is left of their platoon. Misfit's platoon runs back into hiden, using the damage walls for cover. Misfit and Peal rush for cover behind a war damage car. Scorpion: "What went wrong." Combatant (6): "Yea, some plan." Combatant (7): "What's the plan now." Misfit: "That was a great plan Peal, listen stick together guys, we are almost done,...here's other plan." As Misfit tells the plan to Peal and the platoon of combatants, small units of enemy soldiers come rushing out of the large, black, camouflage, brick building. They fire their weapons at the damage walls and cars that cover Misfit, Peal and the other members the platoon. Bullets fly over the heads of Misfit, Peal and the other members of the platoon. Misfit: "Gotta plan guys." "listen up." Misfit tells Peal and the other members of her platoon the plan. Peal: "Everyone got it." The members of Misfit's platoon reply: "Got it ma'am." Misfit: "Lets do this." Peal and the other combatants reply: "Yea, yea, yea, fucking a right." "let's kick some ass." The enemy troops continue to get ever so close to Misfit's platoon. Misfit sees some of the enemy troops reloading their weapons. Misfit: "Now." Peal stands on her neels and fires her weapon into the units of on coming enemy soldiers. Some of the enemy units retreat to the large, black, camouflage,brick building.

12

Peal continues to fire her weapon at the unit of retreating enemy soldiers. The unit of combatants that are with Misfit, hit the ground and fire their weapons. The unit of combatants backing Misfit and Peal, hit and kill some of the enemy soldiers running for cover. The (7) combatant in Misfit's platoon throws grenades and fire bullets with grenades from her m16 rifle. Combatant (7) kills more enemy troops. Unfortunately, she is kill late and taken out of the simulated battle. Misfit continues to fire her weapon, while running for the dead female combatant's weapon. Misfit takes the dead female combatant's bullets and grenades. Misfit: "Sorry," "those are the brakes." Misfit picks up the other m 16 rifle and puts it between a large hole in the wall. She can see everything as she hides behind the wall. She fire her weapon at the enemy troops. She runs behind a car and lays the nose of rifles on an open window of the car door. She starts firing bullets, grenades from both m16 rifles. Misfit, Peal and their platoon continue to fire their weapons. Combatant (5) is killed by enemy soldiers. The enemy soldiers come very close to killing Peal and combatant (6). Peal: "Iam out of bullets and grenades for my rifles." Peal pulls out her side pistol and starts firing. Peal kepts firing as she stand up to charge the enemy soldiers. She kills more of them, not leaving any of them alive. The last combatant (6) Scorpion: "Fuck, where are you Dolan, come back, you are going to get yourself killed." "Dolan, shit."

Misfit: "Cover her." Scorpion goes to sniper mode. He starts shooting and kills more enemy soldiers. Misfit: "Fuck,...Peal, I thought I was the crazy bitch here." Peal: "Motherfuckers,.. come get your death." Peal finds herself in the middle of the killing zone. Peal picks off and kills a few more enemy soldiers, before she runs out of bullets. Peal pulls out her emergency firearm. Peal fires her pistol into the small unit of charging enemy soldiers. She hits and kills more enemy soldiers. Peal falls to her neels, as enemy soldiers bullets fly over her head. Peal kepts firing bullets as the amount of enemy soldiers get smaller. Some of the enemy soldiers come close to killing Peal. One of the enemy soldier almost come very close to putting some bullets in Peal. Peal uses her combat skills to move out of the way of bullets fired by enemy soldiers. Peal manages to put a bullet in the head of the high ranking female enemy officer. She puts another bullet in the chest of another enemy soldier. Peal kepts firing her weapon. Enemy troops kept coming in for the kill. Peal: "See ya homeboy. Peal pistol jams. Peal: "Fuck, fuck me." Suddenly, a heavy sheet of bullets, grenades and rockets come at the enemy soldiers. Misfit running with Scorpion, both are firing opon the enemy soldiers. The enemy soldiers are charging at Peal, trying to kill her.

Misfit: "Peal, laid down, lay down." Peal slowly reacts to the order. There is so much happen around her. Misfit and Scorpion are still firing all their bullets, grenades and rockets into the last unit of enemy soldiers. The smoke and dusk clear, showing that Peal is laying down. Misfit: "No." Fuck no, no please,... don't be dead," don't be dead Peal,... if your dead, Iam going to kick your ass." Misfit runs over to see if Peal is alive or dead. Scorpion stays duck closely behind and down by a wall. He takes cover. He gives cover to Misfit and continue to look out for enemy soldiers. Misfit: "Peal, Peal, Peal,...don't be dead." "Fuck." Misfit gets to Peal's body. She goes to turn Peal's body over. Peal turns over and looks at Misfit. Peal: "Its only a simulation, partner,...tough girl." Misfit: "You are, fucking crazy bitch." Misfit and Peal kiss and hug each other. Scorpion comes out of cover and rush over to the two women. The two look up at scorpion. They give him the thumbs up for okay. Scorpion looks at Misfit and Peal. Scorpion: "Good,...we lived to see another day."Peal: "Nice to see you too guys. Scorpion bend down, he gives Misfit and Peal a hug and kiss, then gives both women a strong hand shake. Misfit and Scorpion help Peal to her feet. The Colonel and Captain Stanly stop the simulation. Everyone claps for Misfit, Peal and Scorpion. Colonel Bender: "Very, very, well done team, or should I say, navy seals. Colonel Bender: "What do you think Captain.

"Captain Stanly: "That was excellent sir yes they work very well as a team, unfortunately I can't say the same for your other military team mates,...Timeworth has what it takes to be a platoon leader." Colonel Bender: "Yes, she does have what it takes to be a team leader." Misfit, Peal and Scorpion, give the Colonel and the Captain a big, yes sir, sir." The Captain looks at the Colonel. Both men look at the combatants that were killed and fail the battle simulation test. The Colonel and Captain Stanly turn to each other, they salute each other, then they salute Misfit, Peal and Scorpion on a well done mission. Captain Stanly: "Ten-hut,...good job guys, fall out and get clean up." Misfit, Peal and Scorpion give a salute and a big, yes sir, sir." The Captain gives orders to the battalion. Captain Stanly: "Good job everyone, everyone prepare to fall out, you are all dismissed." "The simulation is over, return back to your barracks." The combatants that failed the test are given a salute by the Colonel and Captain. They salute back and give a big, yes sir, sir." The failed combatants are given different orders and send back to their military bases. Peal speaks low to Misfit. Peal: "What, Iam chop liver." Just as the Colonel is about to walk away with the Captain. Colonel Bender: "Oh yes,...very good job Dolon, like the way you did that trick, I will see you three in my office,...first, get clean up and report to the Captain." "Once again, very good job people." "Captain.!"

14

Captain Stanly: "Yes sir,…. fall out and meet me in front of the Colonel's office in 45 minute and don't be late." Misfit, Peal and Scorpion reply: "Yes sir, Captain sir." Misfit, Peal and Scorpion fall out. Captain Stanly gives orders to the other gobal battalion members, who won in the simulated battle test, as Misfit, Peal and Scorpion return to their barracks. Captain Stanly: "Fall out and get clean up. All members who won in the simulated battle, will meet in front of the Colonel's office. You have 45 minutes to get clean up, that is all for now people." The winning members of the gobal battalion rush back to their barracks to clean up. Mean while, the losing members of the gobal battalion are given orders to return back to their bases. Peal: "Yes, we did it you guys, we did it,…we should celebrate." Misfit: "We have to meet the Captain in front of the Colonel's office." "Peal, we can celebrate later, besides, we still have the real mission ahead of us." Peal: "Yes, the real mission, that was just a simulation,… listen, suppose we don't…make it." Misfit: "Relax okay, forget I even said that,…you know, we have celebrating to do partner. "After we see the Colonel and the Captain." Peal: "Alright tough girl." Misfit: "Right you bad ass." Scorpion: "Am I invited." Misfit and Peal: "No." "Ha, ha, ha…just joking, why of course you are silly ass." Scorpion: "Lets get clean up, see the Colonel and the Captain, then celebrate our assess off until dawn." Misfit and Peal reply: "Yes, hell yea, alright, party, wow,

wow, wow." Misfit, Peal and Scorpion go to get clean up. The three comrades come out of their barracks. They see platoons from all parts of the military gathering outside the Colonel office. The platoons that were killed and failed in the simulated battle receive their discharge papers. They will be send back to their military bases with the medal of honor. Misfit, Peal and Scorpion kept watching and stoping at the events shown before them. All three continue to walk towards the Colonel's office and pass other barracks. Misfit: "Lets go guys, come on, we can't be late." Captain Stanly: "Good, everyone is here early, follow me, people." Misfit, Peal, Scorpion and the other members, who pass the simulation, salute the Captain and follow him through a large hallway. The Captain salute back, he leads them to large close double doors. Captain Stanly: "Ready guys." Captain Stanly opens the double doors. "Clapping, clapping and more clapping starts immediately after Captain Stanly opens the doors. Clapping comes from Colonel Bender, Captain Stanly, other military personnel, military staff, other platoons and everyone eles in the large meeting room. Clapping continues for all the members of the gobal battalion, who won in the simulated battles. All the platoons from every parts of the U.S military and world military, clap for Misfit, Peal, Scorpion and the other members. Peal: "Wow,"...nice, sweet, wow, lovely." Misfit: "Yea,...wow, ok,...Iam going to get something to drink." Scorpion: "And, I going to get something to eat." "Mummy. "Awesome layout." Peal: "wait up, hey, wait up guys." Captain Stanly: "Enjoy guys, you earn it."

15

Misfit, Peal, Scorpion and the other members, reply: "Thank you sir." Misfit speaks to Peal and Scorpion in a low tone. Misfit: "Yea, thanks,...read my lips, real long party, lovely sir. Captain Stanly: "I hope you do just as well in real combat, Timeworth, there are no second chance in real war." Captain Stanly speaking to himself, watching Misfit. The Colonel, Captain Stanly and everyone greet and shake hands with Misfit, Peal, Scorpion and the other members. The three mango with the other military platoons and guests. Colonel Bender: "Congratulation Timeworth." Misfit: "Thank you sir." Colonel Bender: "You and the others did a fine job,... second lieutenant Timeworth."Misfit: "Yes sir, thank you again sir." Colonel Bender continue to congratulate all the other members of the gobal battalion. The Colonel returns back to Misfit. Colonel Bender: "Oh, excuse me, Captain Timeworth." Misfit: "Excuse me sir, but what did you say." Colonel Bender: "I said....,good job...Captain." Misfit: "Really.....,sir." Colonel Bender: "Really, yes you make Captain, stop by my office tomorrow morning and pick up your bars." Misfit: "Thanks, thanks a real lot sir," thank you sir." "Thanks Colonel." Colonel Bender: "Your very welcome,...really." The Colonel walks away to mango with the other guests. Peal goes over to Misfit. Peal: "Look,... I just spoke to Captain Stanly and...Iam a Captain now." "Ha,ha,ha,ha, laughing." Isn't that great, oh listen, hope this won't change anything between us." "You are still my partner and my girl, tough girl." Misfit: "Yea,...well." Peal: "Listen don't worry, I can speak to the Colonel for you." Misfit: "I am a Captain, have to see the Colonel in the morning." Peal: "Me too, ok we both make Captain, cool, I wonder if Scorpion." Misfit: "Don't you worry now, ok Peal, you are still my partner." Misfit and Peal both hug each other and then salute each other. Scorpion comes over to Misfit and Peal. Scorpion: "Hey guys, guest what." Misfit and Peal, reply: "We know, you make Captain." Scorpion: "Yea,...right, you guys make." Peal and Misfit, reply:" Captain." Peal: "Wow, this is great, l guest, we did a really good job." Misfit: "This is great." Peal: "I know. "Scorpion: "Yea, this is really great, so great, think I am going to dance with that glorious woman, see you guys later." Peal: "See you later tough girl." Misfit: "Where are you going." Peal: "Oh, I and a old friend are hanging out by the bar." "You are welcome to come along, if you don't mind a threeson." Misfit: "No,...go have a good time, don't let me stop your fun, I understand, I am a woman too." Peal: "Ok, are you sure you don't want to come." Misfit: "Listen, I am sorry, Just thought we were going to hang out just you, me and Captain Halls over there." Peal: "Oh,...me, you and Halls." Misfit: "Right. You got it." Peal: "I could cancel my plans."

16

Misfit: "No, don't, go have a good time." "I was just thinking about myself." "Go have a good time." Peal: "Iwill tough girl." Misfit: "Make sure you bust a nut for me." Peal: "Ok,...I think,...oh, whatever that is, see you later." Misfit: "See you later and enjoy." "We will hang tough later, girl." Peal: "You bet ya." Scorpion: "Wanta dance. "Misfit: "What happen to the glorious woman you went to dance with." Scorpion: "She went to dance with that marine over there." Misfit: "Sorry dude, hell no, I don't dance dude, wanta dance,...go over to that chick that looks like a stripper." Scorpion: "Dam, she is hot, let me ask her for a dance, before someone eles does,...wow she real sexy." Misfit: "See, you found your dance partner." Scorpion goes to the sexy woman on the dance floor. Scorpion: "Hi, hi, listen, hello." Misfit jumps in front of the sexy woman, with the tight mini dress army uniform. Misfit: "Excuse me," my friend wants to dance with you." "He was speaking to you." Misfit gets Scorpion a dance partner and a date. Sergeant Karene Stinson:" Oh, sorry madam, sorry sir." "I though you were talking to someone eles, sir." Scorpion: "Listen, relax Sergeant." You can call me Richard." Karene: "Ok Richard and you can call me Sergeant Stinson." "Iam not one of your hoes, do we understand each other." Scorpion: "Oh dam, sorry Sergeant." "Please except my apology, Sergeant." Karene: "Yes, I except your apology, its ok Captain Halls." Scorpion: "Thanks."

Karene: "You can call me Karene." Scorpion: "Ok, great, fine, that's fine with you." Karene:" Yes it is." Scorpion and Karene start dancing in the middle of the dance floor. Misfit drinks and eats, while she thinks of her old friend, lady and her new friend Peal. Misfit remembers all the training, testing and fun times she had with Lady. It is a honor for Misfit to service with Lady, as well with Peal. Peal: "Tough girl, tough girl, tough girl." Misfit comes out of her daze. Misfit: "What,...oh yea, what up Peal. "Dam, are you ok girl, dam, what have you been drinking." Misfit: "I don't know, but it sure beat been lonely,... listen,..Iam ok and yes I had a lot to drink, dam it." "Thanks for asking, you came back." "I thought you were hang out with friends, getting laid,all that good stuff." Peal: "You had way too much to drink tough girl and why of couse I came back to hang out with your crazy bitch ass." "Well, you ready to hang out,..that if you are up to it partner." Misfit: "Yes, of couse you crazy bitch." Some of the guest in the large meeting room, look at Misfit as she carry on. Misfit: "Sorry folks, just have a good time." Misfit, Peal, Scorpion, Karene and Captain Stanly leave the large meeting area, and go off base for more celebrating. Captain Stanly drives them to a part night club/bar and grilL on the island. Colonel Bender also leaves the large meeting area, to looks at and investages Misfit military records.

17

The Colonel looks over and further investigates the training, combat, testing, personal records and files of Misfit's military history. Colonel Bender: "Yes madam, oh right sir, that correct sir, no madam,...yes I see sir, yes, right madam, yes madam, yes sir." The phones hang up. Colonel Bender: "Good bye, and don't have a nice day." fucking assholes." Mean while, back at the club. Captain Stanly: "So, Captain Timeworth, how long have you been in the navy." Misfit: "About 15 years." Captain Stanly: "How long as a navy seal. "Misfit: "Brother, you sure do ask a lot of questions." "What are you writing a book." Peal: "He was just asking a question." Misfit: "Ah,...listen Peal, stay out of this, this dude is asking way too many questions for me." "I wish I would have got laid." Just then, another group make up of rangers, marines, special air force services and members of the army. Misfit: "It's my turn to ask you a few question, Stanly." Captain Stanly: "Shoot." Misfit: "You should be care of the words you chose." Captain Stanly:" What words." Misfit: "like the word shoot." Captain Stanly: "oh, I get it, we are playing some type of psychological game." Misfit: "Call it what you want, well, how long have you been in the navy." Petty boy." Captain Stanly: "I have been in the navy for 19 years." Misfit: "How long as a navy seal." Suddenly,! three of the army rangers from of the group of rangers, marines and special air force services begin to harass one of the waitress in the night club/bar and grill. One of the male members of the army ranger team, reply: "Relax girl, come on relax woman." The waitress: "No," I said stop you asshole, I said stop, stop touching me, you fucking assholes." Two female marines from the group of army rangers, marines and special air force services, join in the harassment party. Two female marines reply: "The man say to relax baby, ha, ha, ha, relax slut, what's your problem. Your our fucking hoe now." Female waitress: "Stop, stop, no stop, I toll you to." Yelling starts." "Yelling and more "yelling follows. The male and female memberof the group fo army rangers,marines and special air force services, reply: "Hey, shut the fuck up and stop that screaming bitch." "You dirty ass fucking slut." The bartender and the other helpers step in to save the waitress from the group of military thugs. Bartender: "Hey, stop, she said stop." "The lady said stop already." "Stop fucking with the help, assholes" The bartender and the other helpers go to stop the group of military thugs. The whole group of military thugs get up and become violent to the waitress. The bartender and the helpers become targets to the group as well. Bartender: "Motherfuckers, come on, I had enough of your bullshit." The waitress yells, yells for help. Fighting starts betweet the two groups of military thugs and night club/bar and grill workers. Waitress: "Stop, help, someone help." Screaming and fighting full the club. The group of military thugs are giving the bartender, the club helpers and waitress a ass whiping. Peal: "I can't belive this shit." "All I wanted to do, is come here for a good time, relax and have some drinks, but look at these idiots fucking the whole night up." "Stop that shit, hey, shitheads." "I said stop the shit, right now." "What are you assholes doing." "Didn't you hear me, you shitheads." Hey, stop already." "Now." Four other members of the group of military thugs, reply: "You want some too, bitch." The others in the group of military ruffians, reply: "Yea, come bring that ass over here."

Captain Stanly: "You want my ass over there." Another member from the group of military thugs, reply: "Your ass is dead, your fucking dead, you and that big mouth bitch." Anyone else want a ass whipping while we are here,...time to get your ass kick." "Sailors." Some of the members from the group of military thugs come to fight Captain Stanly and Peal. Captain Stanly and Peal get into their fighting mode. Misfit: "Yea, Iam right here, you little punk ass bitchies." "Your assess are dead." "Time to get that ass handed to you." "Little punk ass toy soldiers." Misfit, Peal, Captain Stanly, Scorpion, karene and some members of their platoon go into fighting mode. The group of military rought necks let go of the night club/bar and grill helpers.They stop beating up on the waitress, bartender and club helpers. The group come after Misfit and the others. Misfit and her platoon of ball busters go into battle. Blows, kicks and punchs are thrown by everyone involved in the bar fight. The two groups fight it out, to the last person. Misfit takes a ass whiping, but she gives a better ass whiping back. Misfit and her platoon, make up of Peal, Captain Stanly, Karene, Scorpion and the other members of their platoon, win the bar fight. They win the battle, but not without injure. Misfit is hurt. She does not fear pain. She has encounter lots of painful moment in her life. A flash back to her parents and brother's death put her back into the day of her rough child hood. Back to a time of her adaptation by Mary Rollen. Every moment goes through Misfit's head. Misfit still remains aware. Attend and ready for battle. Misfit's platoon does not fear pain or war. They get their asses kick and kick more ass, just the same. Unfortunately for the platoon of military thugs, they get their asses kicked more. The platoon of military thugs lay on the club's floor, in pain, knot out and injure. Misfit: "I thought these punks were hardcore." "The biggest and badest, the roughest and the toughest women and men of the pick." Peal: "I guest not, see what you get, this is what you get when you fuck with me and my platoon." Scorpion: "Good for you shitheads, theres's more where that came from, ha, ha, ha, laughing, uh." Scorpion, still hurting from fighting. Karene: "Yea, oh shit, you okay my sexy boy." Scorpion: "Yea, I been in tougher fights, uh, uh, uh." Karene holds Scorpion around the side of his body. Captain Stanly: "Good work guys, I knew you were the right platoon from the begin." "Ok lets." Suddenly,! Colonel Bender walks into the night club/bar and grill with the military police. Misfit: "Luck for you bitch asses, I didn't kill any of you." Peal: "Ten-hut." Misfit still ready for more fighting. She talks tough, holding a beer in her right hand. Everyone is now standing in attention. Only the knot out, injure platoon of shit heads and Misfit, are not standing at attention. Peal, Captain Stanly, Scorpion, Karene and the others in their platoon, reply: "Timeworth, Timeworth." Misfit: "Shit, Colonel sir, sir." Misfit jumps to attention and drops her beer on the floor. Colonel Bender: "What the hell is going on here." Scorpion: "Oh fuck." Karene: "Oh dear." Colonel Bender: "You people have some explaining to do,… do you all understand."

Misfit, Peal, Scorpion, Karene, Captain Stanly and the other members of their platoon, reply: "Yes sir," Colonel sir." The military police units pick up and arrest the platoon of military thugs from the night club's floor. The Colonel gives orders to the military police units. He gives disciplinary charges to the group of military thugs. Colonel Bender: "Take these assholes away,...now for you guys,...someone explain to me, what the fuck went down tonight." Misfit and the other members of her platoon stay silent. Colonel Bender: "Okay,..no one has the heart or the balls to speak now." Misfit has the heart and the balls to speak for her platoon. Misfit: "I can speak for us." "Colonel sir." Colonel Bender: "Well, speak." Mistit: "Yes sir, we got into a fight with those assholes you pick up from the floor." Colonel Bender: "Did I hear someone say, they got into a fight with some assholes tonight." Misfit: "That me, yes sir, Colonel sir." Colonel Bender: "So, Captain Timeworth, you and your whole dam platoon got into a fight with other platoon." Misfit: "Yes sir." Colonel Bender: "Who started the fight." Misfit: "The other platoon, sir." Colonel Bender: "The other platoon had to be pick up from the floor." Misfit: "Yes sir." Suddenly, Peal, Captain Stanly, Scorpion, Karene and the other members of Misfit's platoon, reply: "Yes sir, that's the way it went down, sir." The waitress, the bartender and then club's helpers tell the Colonel the same story. They also tell the Colonel that Misfit and her platoon are heros. Colonel Bender: "Kept explaining how this fight happen tonight, off base." Misfit and the others explains what happen, step by step to the Colonel. Mean while the waitress, the bartender and club's helpers clean up the mess. Misfit finish talking to the Colonel. She tells her side and her platoon's side of the story to the Colonel. Misfit: "That's the way it happen sir." Peal, Captain Stanly, Scorpion, Karene and the other members of their platoon, reply: "She right, she is a hundred percent right sir, that's the way it went, yes sir, right sir, correct sir," that's right sir." Colonel Bender: "Ok, alright all ready." "Everyone has something to said now." 'Ok, I hope for your shake the other platoon of drunks have something to said for themselves." "I hope I hear the same story from the other pack of idiots." "Do you understand me." Misfit and the other members of the platoon, reply: "Yes sir, Colonel sir." Colonel Bender: "Oh, one more thing,...lam glad your platoon won, fall out." Misfit and the other members of her platoon fall out. They come out of attention and Misfit's platoon breath a sign of relief. Scorpion: Woo,! what a night." Misfit: "We just kick a platoon of army rangers, marines and special air force services asses tonight." "Now, that's what I call a good night." Suddenly, the Colonel walks back into the night club/bar and grill. Colonel Bender: "Oh, by the way, for all of you who like hanging out late." "This night club is officially closed in one hour."

20

"Which mean, you only have one hour to finish your party." "If I come back to this place in an hour and you are still here, you all will be spending your night behind bars." "Do I make myself clear." Misfit and her platoon reply: "Yes sir." Colonel Bender: "Carry on." Karene: "Is he still here, is he gone." Misfit: "Yes, he left, he went out the door." "He's gone now." Captain Stanly: "Are you sure, you are still drunk." Misfit: "Ask the waitress, she will tell you." The waitress: "Yea, he did, just like she say." Misfit, Peal, Captain Stanly, Scorpion and Karene laugh. The waitress, the bartender and the club's helpers thank and show their appreciation to Misfit and her platoon. The waitress, the bartender and the helpers, reply: "Thanks guys, that was some awesome fighting, sailors." "Thank you again, who would have known what would have happen if you guys didn't step in." "Hey, drinks and food on the house." Misfit and her platoon gladly accepted the thank you and the free drinks, and food. 45 minutes have passed after Misfit and her platoon have fought, drunk and ate. Misfit: "Well, it's time to go guys, remember the Colonel comes back and sees us here, we get jail time. "Misfit and her platoon give their good byes and go. The bartender, the waitress and the club's helpers give Misfit and her platoon a good bye and a big salute. Just as the night club/ bar and grill's doors closes, Misfit: "You know what, I should stay, I really like the taste of that food." Misfit goes to open the night club/bar and grill's doors. Her whole platoon gabs and pulls her from the club's doors. Misfit: "1 was just joking guys, come on, it's still early people." "What ever are we going to do for fun." Karene: "Iam definitely not staying here and waiting for the Colonel." "That's for sure." Captain Stanly: "You call this early, wow, it's almost 5:30 am." "Time to get some sleep, guys." Misfit: "I don't feel tried, not one bit, as a matter of fact, feel like staying up for the rest of the morning." Peal, Scorpion, Karene and Captain Stanly reply: "It's so late, it's time to go back to the base and get some sleep." "Yes, it's late." Misfit does not want to sleep. Captain Stanly: "Ok, you don't want to sleep, you still want to have some fun, then let's go back to my place. Misfit, Peal, Karene and Scorpion agree to go back to Captain Stanly's house on the island. Misfit and part of her platoon arrive at Captain Stanly's house. Misfit: "Sweet,...yea cool,nice." Captain Stanly: "Thanks, Iam glad you like it, it's not much." Misfit: "Peal like's it too, right Peal." Peal: "Yes, right honey." Misfit: "Why, Peal you sly dog you, you go girl." Just then, Captain Stanly's roommate comes out of his room. Captain Stanly: "Oh, everyone this is Nick." "Captain Nick Forgos of the U.S marine corp." Deadcold-(Nick Forgos): "Hi everyone, nice to meet you guys." Karene stands at attention when seeing Deadcold.

"Deadcold: "At easy soldier, Relax, your outside the base."
Karene: "Yes sir." Deadcold looks over at Misfit. Deadcold:
"Have we met before some place." Misfit gives Deadcold a, "yea
right, I don't think so Mr," look. Deadcold: "Yes Iam talking
to you, madam." Misfit starts acting silly. Misfit: "He must be
talking to you Karene, or someone eles in here." Deadcold:
"Yes, I was talking to you." Deadcold stands in front of Misfit.
The two look at each other eye to eye. Misfit: "I have seen your
type before,....belive me,.. this is not going any where, it's not
going work dude,..ok petty boy." Deadcold: "Listen, you hadn't
given me a chance, you can't just shoot me out of the sky like
that." Misfit: "Listen, what ever dude." Misfit gives her back to
Deadcold and turns to talk to Peal. Misfit: "So, as I was saying
about the set up." Peal: "So,...you like the set up, nice right,
uh." Misfit: "Yea, it's ok, I think I should get back to the base."
Deadcold: "But you just got here, I want you to stay." Misfit
gives Deadcold a funny, but interesting look.

Deadcold: "I mean…please don't go, you look like a fun person."
"Someone I can hang out with." Scorpion and Karene holding
each other, reply: "Yea, we just got here, yea relax." Peal: "Nick
is a nice guy, give him a chance to prove it." "Come on stay,
relax and try to get to know him, you never know, he might
be the one for you." Misfit: "No, I don't think so." Peal: "You

wanted to party, right…..ok then, here we are." "Please do this for me tought girl, ok you sexy thing, you." Misfit: "Alright,…. alright already." Peal: "Come on girl, let's party." Misfit and Deadcold start talking. After that, the two dance to some music from radio. Peal is happy to see Misfit and Deadcold are getting along. Misfit and Deadcold hold each other as they dance to music. Misfit: "This is only a dance, don't try any funny stuff." "You won't be dance any more." Peal hugs Captain Stanly and Karene hugs Scorpion. Everyone slow dances until Captain Stanly changes the music. Captain Stanly turns the club party music up. Everyone is dancing, drinking, eating and having a good time. Everyone is having lots of fun. Captain Stanly's house is dancing and rocking. Captain Stanly and Peal start kissing. Scorpion and Karene start to kiss as they continue to dance in the middle of the living room. Captain Stanly stops kissing Peal. He turns to Misfit. Captain Stanly: "So, are you having a good time like I promise." Misfit: "What does it look like. Peal: "Good,…see I told you." Misfit, Deadcold, Peal, Captain Stanly, Karene and Scorpion start laughing. Misfit turns to Captain Stanly. Misfit: "Seven and a half years as a navy seal, Stanly." Captain Stanly: "You say something Timeworth. Misfit: "You ask me." Captain Stanly: "You said something, what was that." Misfit: "Yea,…back at the bar, you ask me how long I was a navy seal." Captain Stanly: "Oh right." Misfit: "Remember." Captain Stanly turns down the music, so he can hear what Misfit is saying. Captain Stanly: "Yea right, ok, seven and a half years, alright, good for you,…I knew you were the right person for the mission."

22

Misfit: "Yea, thanks, I know Iam and I will always be the right person for any mission, don't you guys forget that." Suddenly, Deadcold kisses Misfit in the mouth, as she turns her head and look at him. Misfit is a little shocked. She kisses Deadcold back in the mouth. Soon Misfit and Deadcold are making love in Deadcold's room. Captain Stanly and Peal go to the other room to make love. After seeing everyone eles go make love. Scorpion and Karene deside to make love in the living room. Everyone in Captain Stanly's house turns to love birds. Captain Stanly is making out with Peal in one room. Misfit and Deadcold are making out in his room. Mean while, Karene and Scorpion make out in the living room. The music is played lound as everyone in the house make love. Misfit, Peal, Captain Stanly, Scorpion, Karene and Deadcold are very drunk and do not realize they are making out. The next moming, the Light shines through Captain Stanly's house windows, showing it is daytime. Karene: "Shit,...fuck, it's morning time." "Get up Richard." "Get up guys." Karene quickly gets up from the couch and Scorpion wakes up. Karene: "Everybody get up." "Get the fuck up now." Misfit: "Dam,...what time is it." Peal, Deadcold, Captain Stanly wake up. Karene: "We gota get outa here, we will be late for work." Misfit and part of her platoon rush to put their clothes on and rush out of Captain Stanly's house. They quickly head to Captain Stanly's Truck, so that he can drive them to the strategy room on base. Misfit: "Your driving too slow." Captain Stanly: "lam doing 75, besides, I am driving over the speed limt." Misfit: "Pullover, pullover now, dam it." Captain Stanly: "This is my truck, who make you general, Timeworth." "We are moving fast enough, we will make it in time." Deadcold: "Yea Timeworth, just relax, it will be fine. Peal: "Have you see the time, serious, we are going to be late." Captain Stanly: "I don't let anyone drive my shit, this is my truck." Peal: "The Colonel will be very angery." "We will never hear the end of it." Captain Stanly: "Ok, dam, fine." "You wanta drive Timeworth, ok, but don't fuck up my ride." "Seriously Timeworth." Misfit: "Don't worry dude, l will drive her like she my own ride." Captain Stanly pulls over and parks the truck to the side of the road. He lets Misfit take control of his truck. Misfit: "I won't mess up your shit,....your truck." "Okay,serious dude," ah, uh, super charge-v-12-800 horses,... ok, lets see what she can do." Captain Stanly: "My truck, Timeworth." Misfit pulls the truck out of parking and pushs the truck like a road run. Misfit steps down on the accelerator and push on the gas with a heavy foot. Misfit: "Alright, lets see what she can really do." Captain Stanly: "Take it easy with her." Misfit: "Yea,....oh yea, yea, fuck yea, this bitch can move." Misfit drives Captain Stanly's truck like a nasa car champion. Peal, Karene, Scorpion, Deadcold and Captain Stanly are very impress with Misfit driving skills. Both her driving and fighting skills shows she is a expert. Deadcold is impress with all of Misfit's skills. Her driving, fighting, makeout and tough, sexy intelligent ways. Peal, Karene, Scorpion, Deadcold and Captain Stanly reply: "Wow, awesome, cool." Misfit gets to the base, 5 minutes early. Peal: "We could have been late if you drove Stanly." Captain Stanly: "Hey, maybe and maybe not." Misfit: "Here, take back your baby." "That was fun, I like your truck by the way." Misfit pulls over to the side of the road, parks and gives Captain Stanly control of his truck again. Misfit steps out of the truck. Misfit: "It's been fun, but I gota go to work." "Later guys." Peal: "Where are you going tough girl,....where is she going." Karene: "I guest to work." Captain Stanly gets out his truck, runs to the driver's side of his truck. He climbs back into his truck and takes his truck out of park, and he pulls out onto the road. Captain Stanly and Deadcold start laughing at the whole situation with Misfit. Peal looks down at her watch. Peal: "Hey just make it in 5 minutes early, ok that could work." Karene: "You guys think we can get breakfast." Scorpion, Peal, Deadcold, Captain Stanly and Karene reply: "Love that tough girl, yea." The whole team follows behind Misfit, while sitting in Captain Stanly's truck. Misfit runs into the base with Captain Stanly driving into the base behind her. He parks his truck in the parking space nearest to the Colonel's office. The whole team follows Misfit into the front of the Colonel's office. Misfit knots on the office door, Before she and her teammates walk into the Colonel's office. Misfit and the whole team stand at attention. They salute the Colonel. Colonel Bender: "Stand as you are." Colonel Bender salutes back, then drops his salute. Misfit and her teammates drop their salutes and stand at easy. Colonel Bender: "Good morning." "You people are 2 minutes early." "Cutting it kind of close would you say people." "Still early though, it's fine." "The early bird catchs the worm." "All of you should watch your time." "Just remember we are still in the military and on base, unstood." Misfit and her teammates reply: "Yes sir, Colonel sir." Colonel Bender: "One more thing, no one will be charge in the bar fight from last night." "Now, for some more good news, ladies and gentlemen, here are your Captain bars, congratulation on getting your new bars and not being put behind bars." "Congratulation people." The

Colonel salutes Misfit and her teammates. They salute back at the Colonel. Colonel Bender: "Oh yes, take the rest of the week off." Excellent timing, even if you are 2 minutes close to getting your new ranks." "Now, get out my office, that's an order." Misfit and her teammates reply: "Yes sir, Colonel sir." Misfit: "Well,.it looks like the old timer gave us the rest of the week off." "Let's go back to the bar."

Misfit and her teammates get a salute from the lower ranking soldiers as they walk out of the Colonel's office and back to Captain Stanly's truck. Misfit and her teammates plan to head back to the bar, then go back to the barracks to get some sleep. Captain Stanly: "Come on, 1 will give you guys a ride back to the barracks." Misfit is about to enter Captain Stanly's truck, when she hears a familiar voice. Misfit turns to see who is calling her. Lady Commando: "Hey tough girl, hey, tough girl." Oh sorry,.Captain Timeworth,ma'am." Lady Commando runs up to Misfit. Misfit runs to Lady Commando. The two comrades salute and hug each other tightly. Misfit: "Lady,..what are you doing here." Lady Commando: "Well, the Colonel desided to come back to the base, after he drop off some of the soldiers and sailors who fail the test." The Colonel began testing more of us." "To make a long story short,..I passed the test with flying colors." Misfit: "I knew you could do it." "Uh, you ready for some more test." Lady Commando: "There are more test." Misfit: "Yes, you must pass more testing and training." Lady Commando: "Hell, more test, more training." "What the fuck." Misfit: "Hell, I didn't want you to pass the test, but I didn't want to leave you behind neither." Lady Commando: "Wow, some friend you are." "Thanks a lot tough girl." Misfit: "Listen up Lady." "You're here for a very dangerous mission. A lot of us might get killed on this mission, shit." Lady Commando:

"You don't sound too happy to see me." Misfit: "No, no, it's not that, l loss some really close people in the pass." 'You know this." Lady Commando: "Yes I know this, but remember, Iam a navy seal, this is what we are trained for." Misfit: "Listen, l am happy for you." "That great, really happy to see you again girl." "You look great lady." Lady Commando: "Thanks tough girl, or should I address you Captain ma'am....so who are your friends." Captain Stanly: "Ten hunt, stand at attention lieutenant Headman when you address other high ranking officers." Lady Commando: "Yes sir, Captain." "Sir." Lieutenant Nina Headman." "Reporting for dute sir." Captain Stanly: "What are you here for lieutenant." Lady Commando: "I am here because I passed the test, sir." Captain Stanly: "Good for you lieutenant,get down and give me 50 push-up, now lieutenant." "Lieutenant Headman, don't ever let me catch you greeting another high ranking officer that way again, do you understand me, lieutenant Headman." Lady Commando: "Yes sir, Captain sir." Lady Commando salute Captain Stanly and gets down on her hand, and feet. She starts doing push-ups. Lady Commando: "Yes sir, Captain sir." Captain Stanly: "And don't forget to give me a count on each push up, lieutenant." Lady Commando complete her push-ups with no problem and ask permission to stand up. Captain Stanly gives her permission to stand up. Misfit, Peal, Scorpion, Karene, Deadcold stand by Captain Stanly's truck and watchs Captain Stanly disciple Lady Commando on the spot. Lady Commando: "Sir, permission to speak freely sir." Captain Stanly: "Permission granted lieutenant."

24

Lady Commando: "Thank you sir." "Sir, I didn't mean any disrespect to a high ranking officer." "I was just so happy to see my friend, Captain Timeworth, after so long." "Sir." Lady Commando turns her head towards Misfit and looks at her. Lady Commando: "Ma'am, I am sorry if I have disrespected you in any way or forum." Ma'am." Lady Commando walks over to Misfit and gives her another salute. Misfit salutes back and both women drop their salutes and stand at easy. Misfit: "It's ok lieutenant, you can relax." "I give you permission,.... girl, that an order." "I understand your excitement, remember you are addressing an high ranking officer, but we are still homegirls." Lady Commando: "Yes ma'am, I understand lound and clear, Captain." Misfit: "Yes ma'am, lieutenant Headman." Lady Commando picks up her gear and began to walks away. Misfit: "Oh, good luck lieutenant on your training and tests." Lady Commando: "Thanks ma'am." Misfit: "The best luck Lady." Captain Stanly, Peal, Karene, Scorpion and Deadcold tell Lady Commando, "good luck." Misfit, Peal, Deadcold, Scorpion, Karene and Captain Stanly watch Lady Commando and other combatants walk into large black military trucks. Misfit: "Hey lieutenant Headman, need a lift to the barracks." Lady Commando rushs out of the large black military truck and into Captain Stanly's truck. Lady Commando: "Why sure ma'am." Captain Stanly starts up the engine and pulls out of the parking space. Lady Commando: "Permission to speak freely to Captain Timeworth, Captain Stanly, sir." Captain Stanly: "Carry on lieutenant Headman." "Speak freely to your friend, that's your homegirl." Lady Commando: "Yes sir, thank you sir." "So, tough girl, you make captain." Misfit: "Yes." Lady Commando: "always knew you could do it." Misfit: "Thanks." Lady Commando: "It's good to see you again tough girl." Misfit: "And it's good to see you again Lady, let me introduce you my teammates, this is Captain Morgan Stanly." "Who you already had the pleasure of meeting, this is Captain Peal Dolan, Captain Nick Fargos, Captain Richard Halls, and last, but not the lease, Staff Sergeant Karene Stinson." Lady Commando: "Nice to meet you." "Ma'am, sir." "Sir, ma'am." Captain Stanly, Peal, Scorpion, Deadcold and Karene, all reply: "Hi, nice to meet you." Misfit: "Ok girl, here's your platoon and your barrack." "Lady Commando: "Will I see you again tough girl." Misfit: "Yes, I think you better go before your platoon leaves you." Lady Commando: "Oh yea, right." "I better get a move on, tough girl." "Oh, yes ma'am." "Uh sorry ma'am." Misfit: "No need to be sorry." "Now go, see you at in barracks." "Oh, just ask one of the soldiers for me, ok girl. Lady Commando: "Yes ma'am, Captain Timeworth." Misfit: "Oh yea,...carry on lieutenant." Captain Stanly puts his truck in park, Lady Commando opens the truck's right back door and gets out. Lady Commando: "Thanks tough girl, thanks sir, thank you everyone."

25

Lady Commando salutes everyone in Captain Stanly's truck and everyone salutes her back. They drop their salutes, before Lady Commando closes the truck door. Lady Commando: "Thank you tough girl, later." Lady Commando closes Captain Stanly's truck door and races off to her platoon. Misfit opens the front right truck door and gets out. Misfit: "Lieutenant Headman." Lady Commando stops and turns around, she looks at Misfit. Lady Commando: "Yes ma'am." Misfit runs to Lady Commando. They hug, smile and kiss each other on the face cheeks. Lady Commando and Misfitseparate and go their own ways. Lady Commando runs to her platoon. She waves good bye to Misfit, Misfit waves good bye back to her. Misfit goes back to Captain Stanly's truck. She get's in the truck with her platoon. Captain Stanly backs his truck up and drives onto the road. Misfit turns and looks at Captain Stanly while he is driving. Misfit: "Could you try to ease up on my girl." Captain Stanly: "No, I will not." Misfit: "What did you said." "It sounded like no." Captain Stanly: "Yes, no, I said no." Misfit: "Excuse me," she is a." Captain Stanly: "Understand this,..you are a high ranking officer." "This is your rank now." "You are part of a elite military operation." "You should know this from your military training in the navy." Misfit: "What's your point Morgan." Captain Stanly: "What's my point." "My point is this, don't forget you are on a base for the highly trained warrior elite military personal, don't forget your training and all your testing you went through." "Captain." Misfit: "First, don't yell at me, second, get to the point, Morgan." Captain Stanly: "What do you mean, that is the point." "We are not in the street, we are not in a gang or in your old neighborhood, with some gangstar niggers and ghetto bitchs." Misfit, Peal, Deadcold, Karene and Scorpion reply: "Hey, wait a minute, where did that come from." Misfit looks at Captain Stanly with anger on her face. Misfit: "You don't know a dam thing about me,.... stop your truck, stop the fucking truck." Peal: "No Misfit, no." Scorpion: "Ok, everyone relax." 'We are all brothers and sisters fighting the same war." Misfit: "Shut up Peal, You are trying to protect your man and Scorpion." "We are not all brothers and sisters fighting a war." "We are fighting each other in the same country." "Stop the truck Captain, now, before I make you by force." "Morgan." Peal: "Ok, have it your way." "Stop the fucking truck and let her out." Captain Stanly does not listing to Misfit. He continues to keep driving. Misfit: "I will not repeat myself." Captain Stanly: "Fine, you wanta be like that, here get out." Captain Stanly stops the truck in the middle of the road. Misfit quickly opens the right door of Captain Stanly's truck and hops out onto the road. Misfit does not say anything as she walks down the road. Captain Stanly moves his truck towards Misfit and pulls up on the side of her.

26

Captain Stanly: "Listen, I didn't mean to get you upset." "Come back inside Timeworth." Misfit turns her head and looks at Captain Stanly. Misfit: "Yea, I was a hood rat bitch and not a punk bitch, like some people I know." Misfit continues to walk and talk to Captain Stanly. Misfit: "Yes, I make a lot of mistakes in my life and I paid for them." "My parents and my brother were good people,." "Why did they have to die." "Don't think you are better than anyone eles, you shit head." Captain Stanly: "Fuck you Timeworth." Misfit gives Captain Stanly her middle finger and continues walking. Deadcold: "Stop the truck." Captain Stanly: "Not you too brother." Captain Stanly stops his truck again in the middle of the road. Deadcold opens the left door of Captain Stanly's truck and gets out. Deadcold goes to talk to Misfit. Captain Stanly pulls off slowly. Misfit: "Yea, what do you want." Deadcold: "I want you." "Yes you, Captain Timeworth." Misfit: "You want me." "Alright, let's see if you can keep up with me." Misfit races off, with Deadcold hot on her heels. Misfit and Deadcold race towards the barracks, running toe to toe. Misfit and Deadcold get their work out for the rest of the day. Looking outside Captain Stanly's truck. Captain Stanly, Peal, Karene and Scorpion can see Misfit running toe to toe with Deadcold, as they sit in Captain Stanly's truck. Misfit is in great physical condition. She out runs Deadcold by two car lengths. Deadcold: "Wow girl,....man,...you are in good shape,....fucking awesome man." Peal: "I don't think we should ever make her mad again. Karene: "Right." Scorpion: "Yea dude, shit, that is one bad lady." "Didn't she just get out your truck two minutes ago." "Looks like she already ahead your boy and there she goes to her sleeping barrack, with Deadcold three minutes behind her, dude." Scorpion looks at Captain Stanly. Scorpion: "Hey guy, you should have never said that." Captain Stanly: "Probably I was a little harsh in my uses of words." Peal, Karene and Scorpion reply: "No,..really." Do you think so, dude." Misfit takes off her uniform. She leaves her door open to her barrack's room. Deadcold comes into the room and gets a eye full of Misfit's glorious toned hard body. Misfit: "You were already inside me once." "Round two." Misfit drop her uniform on the floor. Deadcold shut the door." Deadcold takes his uniform off and follows Misfit into the bathroom. They make love in the shower. Misfit goes back in her mind to her childhood and teenage memories. She snaps out of her daze, when Deadcold slaps her on the buttock. Deadcold hears the barrack's room door open. Peal, Captain Stanly, Karene and Scorpion enter the barrack's room. Peal sees the two uniforms on the floor. She walks over to the bathroom and knots on the door. Peal: "Tough girl, tough girl, alright tough girl." "We can hear you getting busy in there." Misfit opens the bathroom door half way. She looks at Peal. Deadcold stands behind Misfit. He holds on and feels up Misfit. Misfit and Deadcold are wraped up in a large towel.

Peal: "Oh sorry you guys, I didn't know you were." Misfit: "Relax Peal,...don't have a baby." "Iam pretty sure you seen this before." Peal: "I just want to let you know, that we have no hard feeling towards you. We will be out in the living room just in case you want to talk." Misfit: "Sure, we will be right there Peal." Peal: "Ok, tough girl." Peal goes back into the living room. Peal: "She in the bathroom and Nick is with her." "Uh, oh yes, yes, yes, yessss." Peal speaks silently to Scorpion, Karene and Captain Stanly in the living room. Misfit closes the bath room door. She and Deadcold put on some clothes and she opens the bath room door. Misfit and Deadcold kiss each other on the lips, as they head towards the living room. They come out laughing and playing, like two young teenage lovers. Misfit: "God help us all." "Hey look Nick, it's the welcoming party." Deadcold: "How long have you guys been here." Peal, Captain Stanly, Karene and Scorpion, reply: "Sorry, we are really sorry, really, sorry guys." Didn't realize you guys were getting your groove on, ha,ha." Everyone starts laughing. Misfit: "Oh stop, stop please." "Very funny, get those laughs in." Misfit opens the door to the bed room and goes inside. Deadcold follows her into the bed room. Misfit: "Stop, spare us the bullshit." Peal: "I know sometime, Morgan can be a little bit of a jerk off." "We are turely sorry." Misfit: "I don't need your pity, so stop." Peal: "He didn't mean any of it." "He was only trying to look out for your friend, that's his job." "Don't you believe in forgiving others for their mistakes." Misfit looks through her military gear. She does not pay Peal any mind. Captain Stanly: "Honomessly Timeworth, I am really sorry about hurting your feeling, can you at lease try to forgive me tough girl." Misfit: "Only my friends call me that." Captain Stanly looks at Peal and Peal looks back at Captain Stanly. Captain Stanly: "Well, I tried." Peal turns to Misfit,as she and Deadcold come out of the bed room. Misfit turns on the television. Peal: "You are being a complete jerk now toughgirl." Misfit: "You are not allowed to call me by that name, ever." "Captain Stanly." Misfit stands in front of the bed room door way. Deadcold watchs Misfit and the television. Scorpion: "Sometime we say things we don't really mean." "Didn't you ever say something you didn't really mean, tough girl." Misfit looks at Scorpion, then she looks at Captain Stanly. Misfit: "You said forgiveness, right Morgan." "You know I have not been able to forgive myself, ever since my parents and my brother got killed." "So, I stay in that hiding space." "I couldn't even help them, even if I tried." Misfit starts crying, as she speaks of the death of her family. Misfit: "Ever since than, it hurt me every time to forgive." Misfit becomes angry and very sad, reliving those awful memory. She hurts inside and outside just thinking about it. Captain Stanly: "You are a great sailor, soldier and a good guy." "You are also a great fighter and dam can you run." "Honornessly tough girl." Everyone starts laughing again at the comment given by Captain Stanly. Misfit shows some sign of cheerfulness and happiness, once again. The whole room full with laugher, forgiveness and cheerfulness.

28

Peal: "Yea, I knew you were a great friend, leader and a hell of a better fighter than Morgan." "Tough girl." Everyone in the room laughs at Peal's comment. Misfit: "Alright, alright, alright, alright." "I understand." "Ok you guys." Misfit gives Peal, Captain Stanly, Karene, Deadcold and Scorpion a strong salute and a big warm hug. They give her a salute and a big warm hug back. Misfit: "Yea, you guys are not bad yourself." "You dudes are mad cool." Misfit continues to hug Peal and the others. Misfit, Peal, Captain Stanly, Karene, Scorpion and Deadcold stand in the living room in a big group hug. Peal: "You think we have time for a drink." Everyone in the living room reply: "Yes." Scorpion: "How about sex, we have time for some sex." Scorpion turns to look at Karene and the others. Everyone in the living room reply: "No." Except for Karene, who reply: "Yes." Everyone in the living room laughs at karene's choice of word. Night time arrives. A knot on Misfit's barrack room door comes from outside. Misfit plays cards with Peal and Karene in the living room. Misfit: "I wonder who that is,..oh, know." Misfit opens the door after the second knot. Lady Commando stands at the front of the door with her camouflage on. She gives Misfit a strong salute. Lady Commando: "Lieutenant Headman, reporting for dute ma"am." Misfit is out of her uniform and has her street clothes on. Misfit: "You don't have to do that, come in lieutenant Headman." Misfit hugs Lady Commando with a great warm hug. Lady Commando gives Misfit a great warm hug back. The two best friends in the military hug each other in the barrack's room. Misfit holds and closes the room door. She walks Lady Commando inside the room. Lady Commando is greeted by Peal and Karene. Peal and Karene also have their street clothes on. Captain Stanly, Scorpion and Deadcold are not there. Both men have gone to Captain Stanly's house. Misfit, Lady Commando, Karene and Peal play cards. The four women talk about everything. Later that night,the four women drink, eat and talk about good times. Misfit, Peal, Lady Commando and Karene play fight. They go back to talking about old times. Misfit blocks some blows and shows off some fighting combinations. She hits Peal, then Karene and Lady Commando with some blows. Peal, Karene and Lady Commando are good at martial art. Each women shows off their skills in fighting, but Misfit is truly a great and wonderful skilled martial artist. She has a hard-kick ass heart with the guts and bravery of a Joan of Arc. The brains of Geronimo. She has the attitude and body of a Amazon warrior Queen, all roll into one tough, Smoove and sexy package. Misfit: "Ah, come on, you guys." "I am so tried." Misfit laughs at Peal, Lady Commando, as Karene trys to match her fighting skills. Misfit: "Not." "Misfit throws a few more blows, punchs, kicks and blocks.

She blocks some of Peal's, Karene's and Lady Commando's blows, punchs, kicks and blocks. The three women manage to hit Misfit, but she still wins with superior moves. Lady Commando: "Ok,...you got it girl,.... dam Iam tried for real." Lady Commando laughing and catching her breath. Misfit hits her with play punchs. Peal: "Yea,..you win." Peal trying to catch her breath, along with Karene, who takes a seat on the couch. Peal: "I should have practice before I came over." Misfit, still in her playfull move continues to play fight with Peal. Peal laughing and still trying to catch her breath. Peal: "Stop, ha, ha, ha, ha,..those are not moves, you getting some special training,...someone eles taught you those moves." Misfit: "Yea, someone special." Misfit pauses for a second, she continues play fighting again with her conrads. Misfit: "Come on you guys, is that all you got." Misfit stills blocks Peal's and Lady Commando's blows. Karene sits on the couch and takes it easy. Peal: "You win,...okay, you fucking win." Peal goes to sit down by Karene on the couch. Lady Commando: "Stop, ah, ah, ah, ah." laughing,...ok you win tough girl." Misfit: "You sure you don't want to go another round ladies." "look I will even get on my neels. Peal, Lady Commando and Karene, reply: "No, no more, no thanks,....you got it, for the last time." "You fucking win tough girl." Lady Commando sits down on the couch by Peal and Karene. Lady Commando catchs her breath.

Lady Commando: "Relax, already." Your like a freaking little kid." Misfit stands and looks at the three ladies on the couch. Misfit: "Time to hit the shower." "You three suck." Lady Commando: "You should go shower, you don't exactly smell like roses." ahhh, ahhh." Peal: "Yea, hey speak for yourself." "None of us smell like roses, except for me of course, Iam a rose." "A sweet rose." Misfit, Karene and Lady Commando, reply: "Yea right, ok, if you are a rose, then we must be daisy." "Right girl." Peal: "Let me go shower, before I kick all your assess." Lady Commando, Peal and Karene look at each other. Misfit's barrack room smells like a gym after workout. Lady Commando: "Iam next after tough girl." Peal: "I got third." Karene: "I guest that make me last to shower." Misfit stops in the kitchen and goes to the refrigerator. She pulls out some beers. Lady Commando: "Where the hell is the remote for the television." Peal: "Right here." "You gotta be fast on your feet to get what you want around here." Mistit: "Here, drink up guys." Misfit gives all three women a beer and goes shower. Lady Commando: "Nice." "Mummy, I love a cold beer just as much as I love hot guys." The four ladies laughs and agree on that thought Misfit: "Enjoy, let me go shower." "You guys think you could go other round with me, after I shower." Lady Commando, Peal and Karene reply at the sametime." "No." Lady Commando: "Can you still throw a knife." Misfit: "Can your mother still cook." Lady Commando: "Ooh,..low blow, and yes, my mother can still cook." "She cooks very well by the way." Peal and Karene laugh at Misfit's and Lady Commando's jokes. Misfit comes out of the bath room after taking a shower. Lady Commando goes into the bath room to take her shower. Lady Commando comes out after taking her lovely shower. Peal goes into the bath room next and takes her shower.

30

Peal comes out of the bath room and Karene goes into the bath room to take her shower. Peal: "Shower all yours Karene." Misfit throws a beer to Peal. Misfit: "Heads up." Peal: "Thanks." Karene comes out of the bath room and is the last of the ladies out of the shower. Lady Commando gets up from the couch and heads to the bath room. She closes the bath room door to use toilet. Peal: "So did you and Deadcold have a good time in the shower."

Misfit: "Who,.oh that guy,...why hell yea, he's a hot piece of ass." Peal: "Yea, he is hot, but not as hot as my man. Misfit: "Yea whatever girl, Nick is hot, really hot." Peal: "oooh Nick, oooh yesss." "I miss Captain Stanly already." Peal: "So, do you think Lady is going to pass her tests or even her training." Misfit: "I know she will." "100 percent." Peal: "Some how, I figured you would know, she tough like you." Karene: "Did you see the way she did those push-up." "With no problem." Misfit: "1 could be wrong, thou." "Shes much tougher then she looks." "Don't take my friend for being soft, she not." Peal: "I like Lady too, but suppose she not tough enough for this." Misfit: "You hadn't seen tough enough, unlit you see Lady in action." Peal: "Iet's just get off the subject." "Ok." Misfit: "Did you really have to ask that question." Suddenly, a lound boom comes from outside of the room. Misfit, Peal and Karene hear a loud, disturbing, shatting noise from outside the room. Peal: "What the hell was that." Misfit: "Sounds like a explosion." Lady Commando rush out of the shower half nude and quickly opens the bath room door. She goes into living room where Misfit, Peal and Karene are at. Lady Commando: "I just hear a loud explosion." "What's happening." Misfit: "Be quiet and put the rest of your clothes on." Misfit talks to all four women in a low voice. The lights and electrical power go out. Emergency lights flash red in the room. Flashing emergency warning lights and sounds of danger full the island. The loud noises get closer and closer. The sounds of gun fire and grenades exploding, come from all round the island. The island's military personnel can be hear on the loud speakers. Voices full the whole base. "The base is under attack, we repeat, the base is under attack, we are under attack." "The base is under attack by hostile forces." "All personnel stand your ground." "We repeat, all personnel stand your ground." Misfit, Peal, Karene and Lady Commando hear continuous gun fire, bombing and every alarm on the island. The gun fire and bombings gets closer and closer to their location. Misfit: "Well ladies, it's time to get your weapons cocked and ready." "Looks like the mission came to us." Misfit, Peal, Karene and Lady Commando quickly get into their camouflage gear. The ladies get their weapons cocked, loaded and ready to fight. The island military personnel's voices come back on the loud speakers. Voices: "This is not a test, prepare to fight." "We are under attack." Misfit: "We know already, shut the hell up." "You guys ready." Peal, Karene and Lady Commando reply: "Ready as can be tough girl." Voices from loud speakers: "The base is under attack, all personnel prepare to fight and stand your ground. "This is not a test." The voices on the loud speakers go silent.

Misfit opens the door to the barrack's room slowly with caution. Outside is night and black. Only emergency lights flash though out the base. The lights shine on parts of the base and do not shine on other parts of the base. Misfit, Peal, Karene and Lady Commando come out slowly. Looking at everything around them. They duck down in front and around the door way. Repeated gun fire lights up the night sky. The island's military, fortress, personnel defends themselves against the drug cartel's vicious, murderous and heartless battalion of mercenary enforcers. The mercenary soldiers were send by the Hosts, to kill everyone on the island and in the base. The Alumnus has given unlimted support and orders to the drug cartel, The Hosts.

The orders to send their mercenary army to invade the island's military fortress part base. The mercenary army orders are to clear, kill, rape, torture and capture everyone in the fortify base. Bullets fly every where. Misfit, Peal, Karene and Lady Commando can no longer hear the voices on the loud speaker. Misfit, Peal, Karene and Lady Commando come under gun frre. Misfit: "Take cover and defend yourselves." Misfit, Peal, Karene and Lady Commando take cover behind a large truck and start returning fire. Peal's cell phone ring. She goes into her pocket. It's Captain Stanly calling her. Peai: "Oh thank god, your ok." Peal speaks very silently on the cell phone to him. Captain Stanly: "Good, I was really worried something happen to you." "Iam so glad you are ok, where are you." Peal: "We are by the barracks." "Where you guys left us." Captain Stanly: "Are the others ok." Peal: "Yes,..they are ok." "Where are you baby." Captain Stanly: "We are here with the Colonel." Misfit moves closer to Peal. Misfit: "Who are you speaking to." Peal: "Morgan, they are ok." "They are with the Colonel." Misfit: "Give me the phone." Peal gives Misfit the phone. Misfit: "Let me speak to the Colonel." Colonel Bender: "Colonel Bender here." "Who Iam speaking to." "Make it quick, we under fire." Misfit: "This is Captain Timeworth sir." Colonel Bender: "What's your situation Captain." Misfit: "Sir, there is heavy fighting in the area." "It's hard to make out the enemy from the friendly at this point." Colonel Bender: "Captain, stay where you are and don't move." "We will come get you." Misfit: "Yes sir." The cell phone hangs up. Misfit looks around and at the other three women. Misfit gives the cell phone back to Peal. Peal: "So what did he say." Misfit: "He said to stay in place." Misfit: "The Colonel said they were under fire, that means the whole island is under attack." "I hope Deadcold, Captain Stanly and Scorpion are still alive." "Dam fuckers." Captain Stanly calls Peal again. Peal picks up on the other end of the cell phone. Peal: "Hi, we are ok, the Colonel said to stay here." Captain Stanly: "Yes, I heard him tell Timeworth." "Tell tough girl and Karene," that Deadcold and Scorpion are fine and alive." "Oh, did Timeworth's friend." Peal: "Yes, shes here, with us." "Gotta go, love you babe." Captain Stanly: "Love you, be carefull."

Both Peal and Captain Stanly put away their cell phones. Misfit: "Where can we go to get a vehicle." Peal: "The Colonel said to stay here." Karene and Lady Commando reply: "Yea, he said to stay." Peal, Karene and Lady Commando look at Misfit, as they look at the surrounding battlefield. Peal's cell phone does not ring anymore. Only the ringing from the base alarms, weapons and explosions continuously sound around the island. Misfit continue to talk to Peal, but Peal is having trouble hearing her. The noise is too intense and gets louder. Peal: "What,....what did you say, I can't hear." Misfit: "I said,..where can,..we find a ride,..near by." "We can't wait here,...it's,..too dangerous." "We have to join the,..others." Lady Commando: "Yes,..your right tough girl." "I think it's time to move our assess,... ladies." Misfit, Lady Commando, Karene and Peal stay low to ground and make plans to move towards a vehicle. Lady Commando: "Oh guys, oh guys,...I think we should." Suddenly, more large explosions go off in front of the sleeping barracks. Near by, Misfit, Peal, Karene and Lady Commando move quickly and cautiously through the battlefield. The four ladies stay under cover and protection by a thick, heavy, tall, wide, brick wall. The wall is strong and tough enough to take the bullets and grenades. The military vehicles in the base's parking lots are completely destroy. There is only one car and a half destroy motorcycle in the parking lot that the four women come to.

Some of the enemy soldiers get close enough for Misfit to see. Misfit can see who is firing at her and the others. She can also hear walkie talkie being used. Misfit looks for her walkie talkie and ask the other women for their. No one has a walkie talkie. They have left them inside the sleeping barrack's rooms. Misfit must go back to the barrack's rooms to get the walkie talkie. Misfit tells Peal, Karene and Lady Commando to cover her. Mean while, she goes into the sleeping barrack's rooms to gets the walkie talkies. She rushs out of the sleeping barrack and tells Peal, Karene and Lady Commando where to fire their weapons. The three women take their position behind the wall and find spots where they can see the enemy. Misfit: "Guys." "Look where my head is going,...that's where the assholes are shooting from." Karene fire her weapon at the location of the enemy soldier. She hits and kills two of the mercenary soldiers. Karene: "like,....right there,....and over there." Karene fires her weapon at other enemy location. Killing two more enemy soldiers. Misfit shakes her head to give the other three women a signal. She continue to signal Peal, Karene and Lady Commando about the enemy location. The Three women shake their heads back at Misfit. Misfit goes in for the kill. She kills a platoon of enemy soldiers with in one hour. Misfit joins Peal, Lady Commando and Karene as they fire their weapons at the enemy soldiers. Peal, Lady Commando and Karene see and know where the enemy is located. Misfit makes a other runs into the barrack's room to get more ammunition and weapons. She find them and rushs back out to the three women.

Misfit: "I got them." Misfit gives some to peal, some to Karene and some to Lady Commando. Misfit gives the order to stop firing. Peal, Karene and Lady Commando stop firing opon Misfit's command. Misfit could see the enemy movements. She runs back to the other three women. The ground starts shaking, Through the bullet holes in the wall, Misfit can see a group of large, green and dark orange camouflage tanks rolling up behind the enemy. The tanks are join by other large, green tanks coming out of the smoke, fire and darkest. Misfit: "Shit,.they have tanks, a lot of tanks." "Run, run." Misfit, Peal, Karene and Lady Commando take off running. The four women run over to the next sleeping barrack. The parking lot with the car and half damage motorcycle is closer. Misfit, Peal, Karene and Lady Commando manage to make it to the other sleeping barrack. The large green, dark orange camouflage tanks fires at them. "Boom," the tanks totally destroy the sleeping barrack that they escape from. Misfit, Peal, Karene and Lady Commando are almost hit by the tanks missiles. They nearly meet their end. Peal: "You gave us the signal." "You gave the signal just in time." Misfit: "That's not what I was trying to do." Lady Commando: "Well,..any way....good call, girl." The tanks and enemy soldiers continue to follow and fire opon the four women. Misfit, Peal, Karene and Lady Commando run into other sleeping barrack's room. Other island's military base soldiers are inside. Misfit,

Peal, Karene and Lady Commando speak to the island's military base platoon. The four women and the platoon come up with a plan to battle the enemy soldiers outside the sleeping barracks. All island, fortress and base military personnel are locked in bloody, violent, vicious battles with the drug cartel's army. The drug cartel leader, known as The Host, gives orders to his army from his hiden palace.

Misfit takes charge of the situation and leads a all out assault on the army of enemy mercenary soldiers. Misfit: "We have to try to kill those tanks, before they kill us." Karene: "With what." Peal: "What about calling for our tanks." Lady Commando: "Yea, we can call for a air strike and some of our tanks." Misfit: "I think that's already happen." Suddenly, Peal gets a call from her cell phone. It's Captain Stanly. He tells Peal, he and Deadcold are almost at their location. Fear that the enemy soldiers are listen in on their phone communications. He hangs up the cell phone. Peal: "He said, he's almost here." Misfit, Peal, Karene, Lady Commando and the platoon of island's military base soldiers can hear and see the dragon attack helicopter flying over the sleeping barracks. Misfit goes to the front of the platoon of island military base soldiers and laids down in front of the sleeping barrack's door way. Misfit: "Hi beautiful, nice to see you too,....hand me the phone Peal. Peal hands the cell phone to Misfit, while firing her weapon at the enemy. Misfit: "Morgan, listen up, we are pin down." "Take out those tanks and those bitchies in the middle." "Be careful of the other tanks hiding." Captain Stanly: "Will do madam." Captain Stanly hangs up the cell phone.

Captain Stanly talks to Deadcold in the helicopter. He gives Deadcold orders to fire the missiles at the tanks below. Captain Stanly also keeps an eye on tanks and enemy soldiers firing at them. He moves the attack helicopter up, down, around and side to side. Captain Stanly: "Time to take them out." Captain Stanly and Deadcold take aim and fire missiles, and bullets from the helicopter machine guns. A rain of bullets and missiles hit the tanks, enemy soldiers and what ever is on the ground. Many enemy soldiers are killed, six tanks are destroy. Misfit calls Captain Stanly on his cell phone. Misfit: "Good job guys." "Now, could you clear the way for us down here on land." Deadcold and Captain Stanly reply: "Yes madam, with pleasure." Captain Stanly and Deadcold fire more bullets, missiles and other weapons from the helicopter. They fire tons of missiles and bullets at the remaining enemy soldiers and the four other tanks left over in the area. Captain Stanly and Deadcold keep firing, until all ten tanks and the three platoons of enemy soldiers are complete destroy. Some of the enemy soldiers body parts lay all over the ground. Captain Stanly and Deadcold continue to destroy the platoons of enemy soldiers and tanks with their weapons from the attack helicopter. Misfit, Peal, Karene, Lady Commando and some of island, fortress, military base soldiers continue to fire opon the battalion of enemy soldiers. Soon, Misfit and the others are Joined by more island, fortress, military base platoons, helicopters, tanks and platoons of island military police. The island military vehicle and fighter planes fire on the battalion enemy soldiers, tanks, planes and helicopters. Misfit, Peal, Karene, Lady Commando, Deadcold, Scorpion and the whole island, fortress, military base battalions, squadrons and naval fleets attack the drug cartel's army.

The island, fortress, military base army, Misfit, her teammates, the island's defenders, use helicopters, fighter planes, tanks and other military vehicles, to kill or capture the remaining drug cartel's army. Only a tiny ground force of the drug cartels army escapes. Enemy soldiers who escape from the island and return to the drug cartels, will be killed. Misfit: "I though there were more of them." Peal: "Probably, some of them got away." Scorpion: "Permission to look for any escaped enemy soldiers." "Sir." Colonel Bender: "Permission granted Captain Halls." Colonel Bender uses his walkie talkie to talk to all the island military base personnel on the island. Colonel Bender: "All teams, platoons, squadrons, battalions and naval fleets pursue the enemy forces." Misfit: "Yes sir, with pleasure sir." "I am ready for some more." Peal: "Yes sir." "In pursue of enemy forces." Lady Commando: "Yes sir." "Ready to kick some ass."

Captain Stanly: "Ready to go after the assholes and kick some of assess." The island's military base personnel gives support to Misfit, Peal, Karene, Captain Stanly, Deadcold, Scorpion, Lady Commando and Colonel Bender. Captain Stanly: "Everyone prepare to engage the enemy." Misfit, her teammates, battalions, platoons, squadrons and naval fleets of the island's military base defenses reply: "Yes Captain." Captain Stanly and Deadcold start up the attack helicopter again. Misfit, her teammates and the island's military base army engage the enemy. Captain Stanly gets the attack helicopter lifted into the air for a second attack. Captain Stanly: "Let's go in for the kill." Colonel Bender calls Captain Stanly from his walkie talkie. Colonel Bender: "Captain Stanly and Captain Fargos." Captain Stanly: "Yes sir Colonel Bender sir." "What are your orders." Deadcold: "Yes sir Colonel sir." "What's the order." Colonel Bender: "Wipe, them, out." Captain Stanly: "Will do sir." Deadcold: "Yes sir,.. they are good as dead sir." Colonel Bender: "Good, light up the night sky." "Kill and capture all enemy soldiers." The Colonel hangs up the walkie talkie. Colonel Bender walks over to some of the other island's military base personnel. Colonel Bender: "You people come with me." Misfit communicate with Peal, Karene, Lady Commando and a platoon of island military base soldiers. Colonel Bender gives the island's military base personnel under his command, orders to go ahead of him.

He sees Misfit and walks over to her and the others. Colonel Bender: "Captain Timeworth, this is the real thing." "Are you ready to give orders to a whole battalion of men and women, including your platoon" Misfit: "Yes, I am ready Colonel sir." Misfit tells her teammates, her platoon and the battalion under her command to, "prepare to move out, let's join the others. The battalion lead by Colonel Bender and the battalion lead by Misfit, quickly pursue what is left of the enemy army. Misfit: "I will take the lead." "Let's get the motherfuckers." Misfit's teammates, platoon and battalion give her a big navy war cry. 80 percent of the island's military base defenders are given orders to go after the enemy forces. Some the soldier in Misfit's battalion ask to go ahead of her to give her extra protection. Soldiers in Misfit's battalion: "Captain Timeworth ma'am, we will go ahead of you just in case things get tricky." Misfit: "No,..I will go first." "Really it's better this way. Soldiers in Misfit's battalion: "Yes ma'am." "Ok ma'am." Some of the soldiers look at Misfit as being a little crazy, but she is not. She's got guts and more balls then some of them. Deadcold rides in the back of the attack helicopter looking for enemy trails. Captain Stanly pilots the helicopter.

Along both sides of him are squadrons of attack helicopters. One of the pilots flying the other attack helicopter is Tin Soldier. Deadcold look over at Tin Soldier in the helicopter. Deadcold: "Man, I hear about that guy." "He's tough." Captain Stanly: "Who,..lieutenant Dawn."Deadcold: "Pick up something on the radar." Colonel Bender radios into his battalion, intelligence officers. He tells them to keep going and that Misfit will be joining them with another battalion.

(38) Colonel bender also tells them that Misfit is in command of one of the battalions. Colonel Bender goes back to the base. He takes a platoon of soldiers, tanks, aircraft and other military vehicles, to accompany him back to the military, fortress, base. Misfit, her teammates and her battalion officers, each take a platoon of soldiers, splitting up the battalion. Misfit: "Time to go hunting." Misfit leads a platoon of the island's military personnel, tanks, aircraft and other military vehicles into the middle of the island. Meanwhile, Misfit's teammates, Peal, Lady Commando and Karene lead the other platoons on both sides of the island. Misfit's teammates lead a platoon a few feet behind her and the platoon she leads. They are on a search and destroy mission. Misfit and her platoon catch up with the enemy soldiers. They capture and kill small pockets of enemy soldiers trying to retreat from the island. The other platoons lead by Peal, Karene, Lady Commando and Misfit's battalion officers, help kill and capture other small groups of enemy soldiers and single enemy soldiers. A smaller group of enemy soldiers send through out the island, escape, leaving tanks, military vehicles, aircraft and dead comrades behind. Colonel Bender speaks on the base's loud speaker to his fellow soldiers. He tells them that the fortress, base and island are safe, secure and back in the hands of the island's military. He also tells them, that some parts of the island is still under enemy control. Colonel Bender: "Don't give up the island, don't stop fighting until the island is safe and back under our control. Misfit, her teammates and her battalion and other military personnel reply: "Yes sir,..yea motherfuckers, you fucking punk ass." "Yea little bitchies." "Run home to your mothers." "Yelling." "Cowards, motherfuckers, come back here, come get some." The small amounts of enemy soldiers that escape by water, get off the island by helicopters, speed boats and other water crafts. Misfit,

her teammates, her platoon and her battalion uses their infrared head and eye gear to follow the enemy army boarding the hiden enemy ships at the island's docks. Misfit: "Hand me some of those flares." Lady Commando hands the flares to Misfit. The flares are thrown into the air. The flares drop onto the water. They light up everything in the area, including the location of the escaping enemy forces. Misfit: "There they are." "Tell everyone where the fun is at." Peal: "You got it tough girl." Peal gets on her walkie-talkie. Misfit and the others can see the enemy ships heading for a humongous sea craft in the far ocean. The commander of the humongous sea craft see lights coming from the island and off the water. Misfit can see the humongous sea craft is the size of one football field. The Sea Craft Commander: "Tell the crew to prepare for an attack and take us out of here." Meanwhile, back on the island, Peal talks to Misfit.

36

Peal: "What the hell is that." Misfit:" Well,.It looks like some type of ship." "I want to know who's controlling that monster." "They seem to be very large, heavily armored and arm to the teeth." Peal, Karene, Lady Commando, Mistit's platoon and battalion, also see the humongous monster waiting in the far ocean. Misfit: "Who has some rocket and a rocket launcher." Some of the soldiers in the two battalions reply: "We do madam,...we do Captain,..here madam, here madam." Misfit: "Ok,.those who don't have a rocket launcher, uses your grenade launcher on your rifle, everyone follow me." Misfit and a platoon of soldiers carring rocket launchers and riles with grenade launchers, go to find a way to bord the humongous monster craft. The platoon of soldiers reply: "You see the size of that thing." "They must have thousands of soldiers, sailors, supply and weapons on bord." "Yea, how are we going to take that shit down." Misfit: "Shut up corporal, don't worry so much,...they are already dead." Deadcold and Captain Stanly fly over head. Misfit, her teammates, her platoon and her battalions find water craft at island docks. Deadcold: "Look at the size of her, so they came by ship." "Shit, shes a big one." Captain Stanly: "I thing you better radio this in to the Colonel." Deadcold radios the information into the Colonel. Deadcold: "Colonel, you are not going to believe this." Colonel Bender: What are we dealing with." "Ok, good work Captain Fargos and Captain

Stanly." Deadcold and Captain Stanly reply: "Thank you sir."
Colonel Bender: "Thanks to you two, we will get the upper
hand on these son of a bitchies." "Good job guys, now kill the
rest of those assholes" Deadcold and Captain Stanly reply: "Yes
sir." Deadcold radios into Misfit and the others. Deadcold:
"Time to go guys." "Just got the orders to move in for the kill."
Misfit: "Allright, it's a go." Misfit takes another look into her
binocular." The target is looking even closer then before. Misfit:
"Wait, wait." Peal: "What is it." Lady Commando: "Yea, what
do you see." Misfit: "They are dumping something out of
the ship." The soldiers and sailors on the ship dump the dead
bodies of retreating soldiers. Lady Commando ask Misfit for the
binocular. Lady Commando: "Is that what I think it is." Misfit:
"Yea, probably those magnet should have fought or given up
on the island." Peal ask Lady Commando for the binocular.
Peal: "Yes, that's really too bad for them." Deadcold radios into
Misfit and the others again. Deadcold: "Hey people, we have to
move before they set sail." Captain Stanly: "Let's get moving."
"Move, move, move it, we can't afford to let these shitheads get
away." Deadcold shakes his head up and down, giving a sign
of yes to Captain Stanly. Misfit looks at the distance where the
ship is. She does this for one minute and turns to the others.
She takes a deep breath. Misfit: "All of you are brave to follow
me this far." "Now, let's kick some ass." The battalion of island,
fortress, military base soldiers give Misfit a loud battle cry. They
follow her to the enemy ship.

Every water craft and high speed water craft on the island follows Misfit into the far ocean. Misfit tells the driver of the high speed water craft to go full speed. Captain Stanly radios into Misfit. Captain Stanly: "Timeworth." Misfit: "Yea Stanly." Captain Stanly: "Kick their asses and send them to hell. Misfit with guns loaded and ready for action. Misfit: "Let's get them fuckers." Scorpion sitting beside Misfit. Scorpion: "Going in for the kill." Captain Stanly: "Nick, radio the Colonel." "Tell him to send lots of body bags." "We are going to need them, for these punks." Deadcold: "I will tell the Colonel." Deadcold radios into the Colonel. Deadcold: "He's going to send more body bags." Captain Stanly: "Ok chief, good." Deadcold and Captain Stanly fly into battle. Squadrons of dragonfly helicopters follow Captain Stanly and Deadcold, as they go into battle with the enemy ship. The Colonel is very please. He knows Misfit will get the job done. She is the right one for the mission. Deadcold can hear and see the enemy ship firing it's big guns. Missiles and Cannons launch into the on coming targets. The ship's admiral gives orders to the ship's personnel, to kill anyone that attack the ship. Deadcold hands the radio-walkie-talkie to Captain Stanly. Captain Stanly: "Iam in position." Deadcold: "I got a bad feeling more wars are coming from these people." Captain Stanly: "Yea,...more problems for them." Deadcold: "Yea, I know brother..more problems for everyone." Captain Stanly:

"Keep covering the tough girl and the others." "She's the right woman for this war." Misfit is a mile aways from the ship. Her teammates, platoon and battalion follow her into the storm of battle. Misfit comes closer to the ship. Misfit: "Nice to see you guys." "Time for some pay back." Misfit sees the personnel of the ship already firing their weapons at her and the other hero soldiers. The enemy's bullets fly in all directions. Killing and injuring some of the hero soldiers, as they make their way to the ship. Misfit tells the driver of the high speed water vehicle, to keep her lights off. Misfit tells the other soldiers driving the other water vehicles to turn their lights off. The personnel of the ship must try harder to pick off Misfit and the on coming soldiers following her. Misfit hops off the water vehicle and into the water. She goes under water. She does not fear any bullets, missiles or any other flying projectiles. She continue swims under water, until she gets to the side of the enemy ship. She comes up for air. Watching the crew of enemy sailors, soldiers and look out lights. She also look out and covers her fellow soldiers. Misfit can see the enemy soldiers are looking for some one to try to board the ship. The lights from the ship search for any incoming invader trying to climb aboard the ship. Misfit watchs the enemy ship's lights where ever they go. The bullets and missiles follow the ship's lights. Misfit uses her water-proof walkie-talkie head set to communicate with her fellow soldiers. Misfit: "Guys, watch out for the ship's lights, they see you." "You are toast." "Copy."

She continue to speak very low into her water-proof walkie-talkie head set. Guiding her teammates, platoon and battalion pass the ship's search lights. They get closer to the enemy ship. Misfit and her fellow soldiers continue to fire opon the enemy ship and it's personnel. They kill, injure, hit and surprise the enemy personnel on board the ship. The enemy is destroy with a sheet of bullets, missiles and grenades. Soon, more soldiers arrive from the island's military base, in aircrafts and in water vehicles. They fire at the crew of enemy, mercenary, soldiers and sailors. Gun fire is exchange between the two enemy armies. The night sky lights up with gun fire, the blue water turns to a bloody, black smoked, empty bullet and missiles case of shells.

More enemy, mercenary, soldiers and sailors are injured and killed. The mercenary drug cartel army on bord the ship, is hit with a rain of bullets, missiles, grenades and rockets before they can react. Misfit finds a way to climb on board the ship. The dead bodies of enemy soldiers and sailors fall into the water. Misfit board the ship. A platoon of enemy soldiers run to the side of the ship. They look over board and fire opon Misfit and platoon of hero soldiers. Misfit comes from behind the enemy soldiers. killing them with a hail-storm of bullets. Misfit: "Come on." Enemy soldiers and sailors run up and down the stairways of the ship. Enemy soldiers and sailors race out of the rooms of the ship. Other enemy units come from the deck of the ship. Coming full force at Misfit and the other hero soldiers. Every part of the ship is full with action, as the soldiers from the island, give the enemy army, navy a ass kicking. Misfit goes into killing action mode, using all of her skills and weapons. Misfit weeps havoc on the enemy soldiers and sailors. Misfit gives her teammates, platoon and battalion cover, time and a leave way to get more hero soldiers to board the enemy ship. The platoons of soldiers from the island follow Misfit. They fight their way through the large battle ship. More platoons from the island make their way onto the large battle ship. The Colonel can see the battle intensifying through his day/night binocular. He stands upon a opening in a large military truck. The soldier/driver of the truck brings the Colonel closer to the battle. Colonel Bender can see both forces are taking on heavy damages. Dead bodies of hero soldiers, enemy soldiers and sailors float in the ocean. Lights come from the captain's look out tower on the enemy ship. The admiral of the first enemy ship sends a signal to other water craft. She is a large high speed battle destroyer. The admiral of the enemy battle destroyer and her crew join the battle against Misfit and the other soldiers from the island. Every emergency light on board the first humongous battle ship flashs. The soldiers and sailors on the enemy battle destroyer, fire every weapon at the water crafts from the island.

Colonel Bender gives the signal for a even larger air strike on the enemy ships. Large military combat planes, jet fighters and more combat air craft join the battle. The massive squadrons of aircraft fly over the Colonel's head and truck. The massive squadrons of fighter planes, quickly go into battle. The radios and walkie-talkies on board the enemy's ships full with voices of panic. Our heroine and her brave teammates, the battalion of hero soldiers, and courage of the squadrons of hero fighter pilot's radios, and walkie-talkies, full with the voices of victory. Colonel Bender uses the communication desk in the truck to radio into Misfit and the others. Colonel Bender: "This is the Colonel." Misfit and the other soldiers from the island, reply: "Yes sir." Colonel Bender: "Listen, you have five minutes to jump ship, I repeat, you have five minutes to get your asses off that ship." Misfit and the others continue to fight, while looking for a way off the enemy ship. Colonel Bender: "You now have three and half minutes before that ship is destroy." Colonel Bender hangs up the radio-walkie talkie.

Misfit, her teammates and the battalion of soldiers from the island, pull back. Misfit: "You guys better get the hell off this ship." "Now." Deadcold sees the massive squadrons of military fighter planes coming from the island. Deadcold: "Where did they come from, fuck, what is the Colonel doing." "We told him to send more body bags, not more air power." "Shit." Misfit stays on the enemy ship unlit she is for certain all her fellow soldiers have exit the ship. Misfit: "Come on, move, get off the ship." Captain Stanly flying the attack helicopter, looks down from the night sky onto the enemy ships. Captain Stanly: "Get off the ship." He yells out from inside the helicopter, looking from a view in the night sky. Misfit must cover her teammates and the battalion of soldiers from the island, as they pull back and jump off the ship. Misfit continues to fire her weapons the enemy. She watchs the others jump from the ship. Misfit: "Jump, kept going." Peal, Lady Commando, Karene, Scorpion and some of the hero soldiers, reply: "Come on, come on." Some of the soldiers from the island are killed before they can make their escape. Peal: "What the fuck are you doing.?" Misfit: "Some one has to stay to kill these bastard,..jump now." "I don't know how long we have to they blow this bitch sky high." Peal: "But." Misfit: "No more fucking time." "I will shoot you myself." "Get your ass off this ship, now, dam it" Lady Commando: "What are you waiting for." "Everyone has jump off." Peal takes a quick look at Misfit, then a quick look at the enemy soldiers. Peal turns her head to Lady Commando, Karene and Scorpion. Peal: "Come on, lets go, now." Peal turns her head back to Misfit. Misfit stays cover behind a thick steel plated wall on the ship.

40

Misfit gives Peal a hand gesture to go. Peal: "She will be ok, she cover our backs." Peal, Lady Commando, Karene, Scorpion and a few of their fellow soldiers, jump off the enemy ship. They dive into the water, leaving Misfit on the enemy ship. Peal and others swim to safety. Peal radios to Misfit by walkie talkie. Peal: "Good luck tough girl,.send them all to hell." Misfit keeps fighting until, she sees all of her fellow soldiers gone from the enemy ship. The enemy forces on board the ship find it very hard to kill the escaping island soilders. Misfit manages to keep covering for the escaping island soldiers swimming back to the island. Misfit takes out most of the enemy soldiers and sailors. She manages to move from one point of the ship, to another point. She destroy some of the communication links between the two enemy ships. Unfortunately, Misfit does not stop the communication link from the enemy battle destroyer and the drug cartel, Deathhands. The large enemy battle destroyer moves very far out into the deeper part of the ocean. The drug cartel, Deathhands has manage to communicate most of the messages. He watches what actions took place on board the battle destroyer. He sends the messages back to the Alumnus's hiden palace of operations. The drug cartel leader, The Host receives the messages. Screams come from the palace's walls.

The screams of people being tortured, killed and raped come from the hiden palace. The Host reads the messages send by Deathhands. He hears nothing, as the screams from the victims full the hiden palace. Meanwhile, back at the battle in the ocean, Misfit sees the on coming aircraft. She knows there isn't enough time to waste. She has only a few seconds before the large, combat, fighter planes destroy the one enemy ship. The fighter planes laid down a massive sheet of bombs, rockets and bullets, into the humongous enemy ship. A rain of destruction comes opon the enemy ship. The large, high speed battle destroyer quickly escapes from the battle. The squadrons of island's' military aircrafts kills everyone and everything on board the enemy ship. All pilots of the island's military air force use their radio-walkie-talkies to radio their reports into the Colonel. One pilot after the other, radios into the Colonel. Squadron of pilots: "Roger Colonel." "One of the enemy ship has been destroy." "You can send in the clean up crews." "Your going to need a lot more than body bags, sir." Colonel Bender listen to his walkie-talkie and laughs out loud into the dark, smoked, firely red sky. Colonel Bender: "Good job, guys and girls. Squadron of pilots: "Thank you sir." "Your welcome Colonel sir." Colonel Bender: "See you all back home." Squadron of pilots:" Yes sir." "See you back home, copy Colonel." Misfit swims to a high speed water cycle. She escapes from the enemy ship.

41

Misfit starts up the water cycle and pulls out. Misfit's battalion spots her riding through the damage scenery. Misfit also spots her fellow soldiers and rides over to their small combat speed boat. The battalion of hero soldiers give Misfit, a big battle cheer and a hard salute. Misfit comes closer. She stop the water craft and gives a hard salutes back at her battalion. Misfit: "Did you miss me." "1 was only gone for four minute." "Ok, let's move out." The small combat speed boat, half full with hero soldiers from the island, follow Misfit back to the island. The Colonel waits for Misfit and the rest of the hero soldiers to come back to the island. Colonel Bender stands next to a large military truck. He looks through his binocular. Misfit comes up in the Colonel's view. She is driving the water cycle at a high speed. The small combat speed boat with hero soldiers ride beside her. Colonel Bender walks away from the truck. A platoon of military medical personnel help injured, as they make it back to the island. A platoon of military police wait by the Colonel's truck and along island's front. The Colonel walks up to Misfit and the others. Misfit rides the water cycle onto the island's front. She stops the water cycle and get otf. Misfit salutes Colonel Bender. The other soldiers from the island stop the small speed boat at the island's front. They hop off the small combat speed boat and walk onto land. They walk up to Misfit and stand beside her. They give Colonel Bender a salute. Colonel Bender: "Well,.nice to see you are still among the living." "Captain Timeworth." Misfit: "Well, it's nice to see you too Colonel sir." Colonel Bender: "I see you are still a smart ass." "Good,..Misfit." Misfit: "What did you call me, sir." Colonel Bender: "You hear me Captain."

"I call you Misfit." Misfit: "No one knows me by that name, unless I tell them."Colonel Bender: "Yes, I seem to remember a particular navy staff sergeant." "Mummy, what was her name." "Oh yes, Mary Rollen, that it, yes Mary." "Does the name bring back memory." Misfit: "Sir." "Your crossing a dangerous road. Colonel Bender: "Oh really, Captain Michelle Misfit. Timeworth." "The little girl who parents and little brother were murder by a vicious drug dealer." "Later after, she was put up for adopt." "Join a vicious street gang and was taken in by Mary Rollen, isn't that right Misfit." Misfit: "Sir, you are." Colonel Bender: "Am I, now, is this right or wrong Captain.! "Misfit: "Really sir,...you have no right to." Colonel Bender: "Captain, come with me." Misfit: "Is that an order sir." Misfit looks at the Colonel with anger and mistrust on her face. She shows no fear of him. Her teammates and some of the battalion hero soldiers, look opon Misfit with a little confusion. Colonel Bender: "Yes that an order Captain." Colonel Bender calls out to the military police platoon and gives them orders to arrest Misfit. Colonel Bender: "MPS, place this women under arrest and take her to the truck." Military police: "Yes sir." Colonel Bender looks at Misfit. Colonel Bender: "If you resist, you will be shot." "Go ahead, resist."

The military police platoon escort Colonel Bender and Misfit to the large truck. The Colonel, Misfit and some of the military police, get into the large truck. Misfit's teammates and some of her fellow soldiers remain in a state of confusion. The Colonel puts his head out the window. Colonel Bender: "Corporal, let's get a move on." The Corporal Driver: "Yes sir." The corporal drives the large black military truck a few feet, after being stopped by the crow of island soldiers. The platoon of military police cars following behind the large black military truck, stops. Peal: "What just happen." Deadcold and Captain Stanly land the helicopter a few feet away from a platoon of soldiers and some military vehicles. They run out of the helicopter and race to Peal, Scorpion, Karene, and Lady Commando. Deadcold: "This is a joke, right, right." Colonel Bender: "I am not fucking joking, move." Deadcold, Captain Stanly, Karene, Scorpion, Peal, Lady Commando and some of her fellow soldiers stay standing in front of the large black military truck. Colonel Bender: "I will not ask again, everyone get the fuck out of the way." Misfit starts laughing at the Colonel. He trys to get Misfit's teammates, her battalion and some of the other soldiers to move out of the way. Misfit: "Ha, ha,..Colonel, you really know how to show a girl a good time." "It's only been our first date." Colonel Bender tells the corporal/driver to use the radio-walkie-talkie, to tell the platoon of military police to clear the way for the truck. Colonel Bender: "You think this is a joke." "Young lady, this is not a date."

"You are going to jail for a long time." Colonel Bender puts his head out the window again. Colonel Bender: "Get back from the vehicles." "You fucking assholes, that an order." Captain Stanly takes a quick look at Deadcold and looks back at the truck carrying the Colonel and Misfit. Captain Stanly: "Let's go Nick." "You guys, move out the way." "Got dam-it, move out, you hear the man." Let's go, move, obey the Colonel." "Move now." Captain Stanly takes out his gun and fires four shots into the air. The large angry crow of island soldiers make room for the truck and the platoon of police cars to pass. Misfit: "It looks like you got what you wanted, sir,..so what do you want from me." The Colonel looks at Misfit with a wondrous expression. He gives the corporal/driver the signal to move the truck again. The platoon of military police get back into their cars and continue following the large black military truck. Meanwhile, Misfit's teammates, her battalion and some of the island soldiers, talk about Misfit's actions.

Captain Stanly: "Who ever she is, she sure is brave." Peal: "That was crazy, but excellent." Lady Commando: "Yea, she always seens to do such a great job." Scorpion: "Cool,...so cool, fucking A-right, man." Deadcold: "You know, that was really cool." "She is freaking so hot." "Really hot,..Iam really falling in love with that woman." Lady Commando:" We know already guy." "I meant sir." Deadcold: "It's alright, your cool with us in my book." "I like the way you wiped ass, out there, sergeant." Lady Commando: "Thanks sir." Scorpion: "Good job sergeant." Lady Commando walks to the large camouflage military transport with Peal, Karene, Scorpion, Deadcold, Captain Stanly and some other soldiers. Lady Commando, Peal, Karene, Scorpion, Deadcold, Captain Stanly get into the military transport. Lady Commando looks outside the windows of the military transport. Meanwhile, Deadcold, Karene, Peal, Captain Stanly, Lady Commando and Scorpion think about Misfit. They think about the way she fought and killed many of the enemy soldiers and sailor. A army of tanks, large camouflage military transports, military trucks, military aircrafts and all other military vehicles, return back to the humongous hiden fortress in the middle of the island. The large black military truck carrying the Colonel and Misfit, rides into the fortress/ base. Colonel Bender and Misfit get out of the truck. The corporal/driver pulls off. He parks the truck in a large parking space. The military police retain and keep Misfit under arrest. Misfit is a tough woman. She desides not to go with the Colonel and the platoon of military police. She will give them a fight. As part of the platoon of military police go to park their cars. Misfit: "Not so fast fellow." Some of the platoon of military police officers try to retain Misfit. She goes into action like a hurricane ripping through a town. Misfit: "Hands off you jerk." Misfit gabs, grips, tums, trips, blocks, throws blows, kicks and punchs. Some of the platoon of military police officers get their asses kick. Soon the other military police officers come to try to put Misfit down on the ground.

The platoon of military police use brutal force, to try to retain Misfit. Misfit shows, the harder they come, the harder they will fall. Misfit is extremely skilled and trained so harden, that the platoon of military police are taken down. Lady Commando, Peal, Deadcold, Captain Stanly, Karene, Scorpion and some of their fellow soldiers ride into base. They can see from the truck's windows, Misfit fighting and kicking the platoon of military police assess. Lady Commando: "Hey,..they are jumping Timeworth." Scorpion: "Shit, that's not fair." Misfit's teammates and some of her fellow soldiers, tell the driver to stop. The driver of the truck stops. Misfit's teammates and some of her fellow soldiers, race out of the military transport. They races to Misfit rescue. Other units of military police race to help their fellow mp, to put Misfit down on the cold, concrete, base ground. Our hardcore fighting female heroine, keeps fighting the on coming military police units. The platoon of military police finds it, even harder to take down Misfit. Soon, Peal, Scorpion, Karene, Deadcold, Captain Stanly, Lady Commando and some of their fellow soldiers join the fight. Misfit, her teammates and her fellow soldiers beat up and kick the shit out of the platoon of military police. The Colonel gives a order to the sergeant in the MP platoon. Colonel Bender: "Sergeant." "Retain and arrest all of them, right now." The platoon of MPS can not retain or bring Misfit to her neels. They find it harder to follow orders from the Colonel, as they fight with Misfit, her teammates and some of her fellow soldiers. They continue to fight along side her. Other platoon of MPS come to join in the fist fight. Colonel Bender has seen enough. He pulls out his pistol. He fire four shots into the air, to bring the fighting to an end. Misfit laughing and fighting. Misfit: "Come on you fucking bastards." Misfit, her teammates and some of her fellow soldiers fight more and more with the two platoon of MP. Misfit continues to fight harder and harder. She continues to beat up on the group of military police officers. Misfit: "Wanta go another round." Misfit keeps fighting, even as Colonel Bender fires four shots into the air. She has been knot down, knot out, hurt in many battles, dragged on the grounds of the world. She wasn't going to let a small army of MP bully her, now. The Colonel fires his pistol into the air. Colonel Bender: "Enough." "Shes one dam woman, stop fighting." The Colonel fires other four more shots into the air, from his semi-automatic pistol. He fires other shot into the air again. Misfit: "You guys fight like little pussies." Misfit still stands on her toes, as she spits blood from her mouth. Misfit get's time to rest from the hard fight. Misfit: "I gave you guys a ass kicking in front of your chicken shit Colonel." The Colonel points his pistol at Misfit. He stops himself from putting a bullet into her. Misfit becomes all excited from fighting. All the fighting makes her want to fight to the death. Misfit: "You guys should have been faster." "You gota hit me harder then that." "That definitely wasn't good enough fellows." Misfit stands ready to fight again. She

94   RODNEY S. CAMPBELL

takes a look at the Colonel. Misfit: "Come on, is that all you got Colonel." Colonel Bender: "You crazy fucking bitch." The Colonel trys to fire at Misfit, but Misfit is still fast enough to take out her hiden combat knife.

She throws the knife directly into the Colonel's pistol hand. Misfit ducks down into a safe position. The bullet from the Colonel's pistol, miss Misfit by inchs. Misfit comes out of her ducking position. She charges at the Colonel. The platoons of MP pull out their guns. Some of the MP rush to the military patrol vehicle, to get rifles. They don't get the change to fire their weapons, thanks to her teammates, and some of her fellow soldiers. She has some good comrades on her side. Misfit attacks the Colonel, while her teammates and some of her fellow soldiers attack the platoons of military police. The battle is back on. Combat platoons and military police platoons throw blows, punchs, kicks, blocks, gabs. Some of the members of the combat platoons and military police officers platoons, fight the same way they are trained. The Colonel is no whimp or coward. He has a few self defense moves of his own. Misfit and Colonel Bender go toe to toe, blow for blow and kick for kick. Colonel Bender: "You crazy bitch,..your going to pay." The Colonel and Misfit fight like two caged fighter. The fighting becomes more out of control. Colonel Bender knows he must put a stop to Misfit, before some one get's killed. Colonel Bender manages to do a combat move on Misfit. He blocks her blows, knots her to the ground. The Colonel finds his pistol. He picks up the pistol from the ground, before Misfit or any of her comrades can stop him. Colonel Bender uses his other hand to fire a warning shot at Misfit. He only wants to frighten her and to make her stop fighting. Colonel Bender fire other warning shot from his pistol. The bullet goes into the ground next to Misfit. Colonel Bender uses his pistol to keep an aim on Misfit. Colonel Bender: "If she attempt to get up from the ground, I will put a bullet into that hard head yours. Colonel Bender: "Stop." I won't hesitate to kill you." "You dam bitch." "I will have the rest of you arrested for helping this war criminal." Do I make myself clear." Misfit's teammates, Peal, Karene, Deadcold, Captain Stanly, Lady Commando, Scorpion, and some of their fellow soldiers, stop fighting the platoons of MP. Misfit stays on the ground, as the Colonel talks. Colonel Bender: "Look at you dam fools." "You ready to kill each other over her." "Give the MPS back their weapons." "Down on the ground and give up, now." I will only say this once." I will charge you all with mutiny, if you do not obey my orders." Everyone is looking at the Colonel pointing his weapon at Misfit. Misfit, her teammates and her fellow soldiers, stop fighting the platoons of MP. They give back the weapons they took from the MPS. Colonel Bender and the platoons of MPS take control again. Colonel Bender: "You." "Captain Timeworth, get up, let's go."

45

Misfit gets up from the ground, not having a choice in the matter. She is placed unarrested and taken in by a platoons of MPS. Colonel Bender: "Anyone eles want to be locked up." Everyone involved in the fight along Misfit, do not answer back to the Colonel. Colonel Bender: "I didn't think so,.now carry on." Misfit is taken away in handcuff by the platoons of MPS. She is escorted to the military prison on the base. Meanwhile, Misfit's teammates and some of her fellow soldiers can only witness Misfit being taken away. Colonel Bender: "Your going to spend a lot of time behind bars for this Timeworth." Misfit: "Fuck you asshole." The Colonel punchs Misfit in the stomach.

She bends just a little and stands straight again. She spits out blood, laughing at Colonel Bender. Peal: "Hey, that's brutality." Lady Commando: "Fuck this shit, that's not right." Captain Stanly: "What the hell was that for." "Colonel." Deadcold and Scorpion both reply: "Hey, that's no way to treat a hero." Karene watching the situation along with the other soldiers. Karene: "Assholes, take it easy Colonel,sir." Colonel Bender turns his head to look at Karene. Colonel Bender: "Speak only when given orders by me or a superiors, is that clear soldier." Karene: "Yes sir, colonel sir." Colonel Bender: "Get back to the office staff sergeant Stinson." The rest you get out of my sight! Karene: "Yes sir." As Misfit is being taken away to the military jail, her teammates and some of her fellow soldiers become hostile. They begin moving towards Colonel Bender and the platoons of MP. The Colonel warns them to stay back. He tells the platoons of MP to keep moving Misfit to the vehicle. Colonel Bender: "Don't even think about it,...go ahead, try me." Colonel Bender holds and aims his pistol at Misfit's head. Colonel Bender: "Iam not joking, stand down." The platoons of MP keep their weapons drawn at the crow of angry soldiers, as they keep moving Misfit closer to the military vehicle. They protect the Colonel and keep an eye on the crow of angry soldiers. The crow of angry soldiers stay around and follow the Colonel. while the platoons of MP escort Misfit into vehicle. Colonel Bender: "I will put a bullet in everyone of you, if you don't back off." I will have you arrest for assaulting an officer." The platoons of MP ready themselves to arrest any soldier, who does not obey the Colonel's orders. Colonel Bender: "Back away, that's an order, dam it, do you understand." Captain Stanly watchs the Colonel and the platoons of MP becoming nervous. They look like they want to shoot everyone.

46

Captain Stanly: "Stand down you guys, he means it, stay hell out of it, Stand down and follow orders, there's nothing more we can do." "It's out of our hands." Misfit's teammates, and some of fellow soldiers come to their sense and calm down. Captain Stanly: "It's time to go back to work people." let's go, let's go." Colonel Bender watchs and walks with the platoons of MP. They escort Misfit into the military vehicle and off to the military jail. Colonel Bender speaking silently to himself while inside military vehicle. Colonel Bender: "Good,...go back to work." Colonel Bender watchs the crow of angry soldiers from the moving vehicle. Captain Stanly: "Time to go, let's go you bunch of maggot." "Now, let it go, move out." Deadcold speaking silently to himself. Deadcold: "It's alright." It's ok, for now." Captain Stanly still talking to his comrades. Misfit's teammates and her fellow soldiers break apart. They go back to their military jobs. Colonel Bender walks into the military jail with Misfit and a platoon of MP escorting her. Colonel Bender: "Lock that fucking crazy bitch in the cell." "Iam going back to my office sergeant." Mp Sergeant: "Yes sir, Colonel sir." Colonel Bender walks out of the military jail and walks back to the truck. The corporal/ driver opens the left door of the truck from the inside. The Colonel climbs into the truck. The corporal /driver and the Colonel pull onto the road. They head back to the Colonel's office. The unit of MPS put Misfit through hell. Four MPS take Misfit to a room in the military jail. They have her remove her combat uniform. They give her a cold shower with a water holes. She is put into a military jail house, orange uniform. One of the MP takes the handcuffs off and push her into a small jail cell, and lock it. Colonel Bender tells the corporal /driver to stop and turn the truck around. They go back to the military jail house. Colonel Bender shows up at the front of the jail house. He walks into the jail house to say something to Misfit. Colonel Bender walks up to the jail cell holding Misfit. He has forgotten to tell Misfit her rights. Colonel Bender's plan for revenge has make him forget a lot. He takes away Misfit's rank as an Captain. Colonel Bender: "You are a great disappointment to me." "A insubordinate military personnel get death for what you did." Misfit locked behind the bars of the jail cell, just watchs the Colonel talk bullshit. Colonel Bender: "You are lucky, girl, I still like you Timeworth. Colonel Bender turns his head away from Misfit. He looks at the four mps guarding Misfit. Colonel Bender: "Make sure you keep a close eye on her, she a vicious one. The Colonel turns his head back to look at Misfit. He quickly jumps back against the jail house wall.

Misfit gets up quickly and silenly from sitting down on the bed in the cell. Colonel Bender gets the shock of his life. Colonel Bender: "Dam, Fuck, shit." "Watch her,..she's all your, keep your eyes on her Captain, understand me." Mp Captain: "Yes sir, Colonel." The Mp Captain tells the four mps guarding Misfit, to watch and guard her well. The Mp Captain gets on his walkie talkie. Mp Captain: "Open the gates to the halls of cell-D, lower level." Mps in the jail house control room reply: "Yes sir." As Colonel Bender and the Mp Captain exit the halls, the four mps guarding Misfit, push her back from the bars of the cell by using their knight sticks. Colonel Bender and the Mp Captain take the elevator up. The thick steel gates closes back on remote control from the mps in the jail house control room. Meanwhile, in the elevator. The Mp Captain tells Colonel Bender, "it was much too dangerous to for you to be around Timeworth. The four Mps tell Misfit to stay away from the bars of the cell. Misfit move to the middle of the small jail cell. She looks at the four mps through the cell bars. Misfit: "Ah, did you have to take the handcuffs off." "You really should have left them on dudes." The four mps laugh at Misfit. They walk away through the open thick steel gates. The gates close and lock back behind them. The four mps go into the elevator. Misfit settles down, as she is left along. She sits down, thinking on the couch in the quiet cell. Misfit gave the four mps a very hard time going into the cell. The four mps had to push, gab and knot her into the cell. The large, thick, steel gates open. One of the mp walk in with a tray of food. He goes to the small opening in the bars of the cell. The mp pushs the tray of food through the opening. Misfit: "This cell is a little too small for me." "You should let me out, so you and I can get busy homeboy. The mp looks at Misfit with a serious face. Military Police(1): "Your ass is lucky you didn't die today,..you crazy bitch." The mp quickly puts his right arm through the small opening in the bars.

He takes back the tray of food and begins to eat the food. Military Police(1): "Uh, uh, looks like you just miss out on dinner, breakfast and lunch." Misfit looks at the mp. Imagines of kicking the mp's ass come to her mind. Military Police(1): "Breakfast will be serve in the moming." He laughs at Misfit and walks away. The mp uses his walkie-talkie to radio into the mps in the control room of the jail. Military Police(1): "Sergeant Rodriguez just finish feeding the prisoner." "Open the gates." The mp walks through the open gates. The gates close back behind him. Misfit quickly gets up from the bed and goes to look at the mp going through the gates. The mp goes upstair through the stairway. Ten minute pass and another mp comes. The gates open. She stands at the front of Misfit's jail cell. Military Police(2): "You better learn how to talk to us." "You fucking street bitch." "Understand."

48

Misfit stands at the front of the jail bars on the other side of the cell. She tells something to the mp. Misfit: "Come closer to the bar, I couldn't hear you sergeant." Military Police(2): "What was that." Misfit: "You hear me the first time." Military Police(2): "Alright." "I will come closer." The mp comes closer to the cell bars. Military Police(2): "I said, you, choking sound." Misfit grabs the mp by the throat and right breast. She applys pressure onto the mp's throat and right breast. Misfit makes it hard for the mp to breathe. Misfit: "I can hear you now." "Stupid." Misfit increases her choke hold, while at the same time, she increases her grip on the mp's breast. The mp desperately trys to break free of Misfit's death grip. Misfit: "Oh,..and yes, I do know how to talk to dick heads,.... tell me, how does it feel to know you are about to die." The choking mp manages to hit her emergency button on her walkie-talkie. The help alarm goes on upstairs in the control room. A unit of mps hear the alarm on the top level of the military jail house. The unit of mps in the jail house control room and the units of mps in the military police station, quickly respond to the emergency. Mp Captain: "Oh shit, sergeant jameson is in trouble." "Move out." Soon, other mps come to open the gates leading to the hallway of jail cells. Units of mps also come from the military police station. The other mps rush through the gates to help the female mp sergeant. The small group of mps grab a hold of Misfit's arms.

They try to pull her off and losen the hold Misfit has on the mp. Misfit: "Now, this is fun," ah, ah, laughing at the mps." One of the mps grabs a tap-stun-gun from her pistol belt. She zaps Misfit on the right shoulder. Misfit jerks somewhat from the small volts of electricity go through her body. Misfit laughing out loud. Misfit: "Ah, ah, ah, ah,...feels so fucking awesome." "Feels fucking good." The small group of mps stun and zap Misfit with more volts of electricity. Misfit: "Fuck me good, ah, ah, ah, ah, yea come on big dad." After zaping Misfit with even more power from the stun guns. The small group of mps use their knight sticks to knot Misfit out cold. They knot her out cold to the cell floor. They push, pull, kick and punch Misfit continuously.

She falls to the jail cell floor. The female mp sergeant that Misfit grabbed, falls to her neels. She catchs her breath. The unit of mps take on injured as they beat up Misfit. The shaken female mp sergeant is taken to the island's military hospital. Meanwhile, Misfit lays unconscious on the jail cell floor. Two mps stay behind to open Misfit's jail cell. They drag the unconscious Misfit and put her on to the jail cell bed. The two mps lock Misfit's jail cell. They keep a watchfull eye on Misfit. Morning time arrival. The two mps have left Misfit unconscious on the jail cell bed. It is five o'clock am and dawn is coming.

49

Misfit is awakening by feet steps of a unit of mps. Misfit stays on the jail cell bed. Her eyes closed, but she is awake. Back at the Colonel's office. Colonel Bender: "Yes madam,...yes madam,...yes, it's her,...that's correct madam,....no sir,....no I did not tell her anything,...no sir,...right sir,...understood,...yes sir." Colonel Bender sits at his desk looking over a report send by the alurnnus. Colonel Bender: "Yes madam, I know,....very well madam,...yes sir, good,...thank you sir, thank you madam." The phone hangs up. Colonel Bender hangs up his phone. He picks up his phone again. He puts a call into all the company battalion's commanders. Colonel Bender: "It's time for the mission to began." Captain Stanly and Deadcold play cards in the island's hiden military airport hangar. Captain Stanly gets a call from one of the phones in the hangar. Captain Stanly turns his head to look at Deadcold. Captain Stanly: "Commander Donald James just call,...the mission has began." Peal gets a call from Deadcold. Peal: "It's time." "Dam." "No tough girl to watch our backs." Deadcold: "No." "No tough girl, right." Peal and Deadcold hang up their phones. Peal calls Lady Commando. Peal: "Time for the mission." Lady Commando: "What mission, what's happening." Peal:" I just got a call from Captain Stanly. The top brass are starting the mission, we have been training for, understand lieutenant." Back at the island's military jail house. A unit of mps open Misfit's jail cell. The unit of mps go into Misfit's jail cell. Military Police Officers: "Get the fuck up." "Good morning bitch." Time to get your ass up off the bed." "You motherfucking bum." They tap her with their baton, but Misfit just laid unresponsive. The mps leave the Misfit's jail cell open. Male mp sergeant: "She's out cold." "You four shouldn't have a problem with her now." The male mp sergeant leaves four mps to take care of Misfit. The four mps go on each side of the jail cell. They go closer to check out Misfit's condition, as she laids monitionless on the jail cell bed. The four mps hit, tap, push, pull and kick Misfit. She does not respond to the mps. The four mps go back to hitting, tapping, pushing, pulling and kicking her harder. Suddenly, Misfit jumps into action. She grabs, blocks, pulls, pushs, punchs and kicks at the four mps. Her hard blows hit and knot the four mps down to the jail cell ground. Misfit blocks blow after blow deliver by the four mps. Misfit returns with hard, quick, powerful blows to the faces and bodies of the four mps. Misfit always takes a beating and comes back kicking ass. Misfit takes out, puts down and knots out the four mps.

She Makes sure the jail house cameras catch nothing. Misfit: "Nightly, nightly boys and girls." Misfit stays off the jail house cameras view. The four mps stupidly leave the large, thick gates open. Misfit makes her way out the jail cell and into the jail cell hallway. She pass the large, thick gates, and into the stairway. She goes upstair to the military jail house control room. Misfit stays hidden behind the double front doors of the control room. She quickly makes her way to one of the front desk in the control room. She stays hidden from the mps. Misfit can see some of the mps with their captain and where they store their weapons. Some of the mps are sitting down at their desk and talking. The other mps take orders from the captain. One of the mps walk to the front desk. Misfit jumps up and hit's the mp with a powerful blow to the face. Knotting him unconscious and over the desk. He falls onto the floor. Other mp comes through the double front doors. Misfit grabs and pulls the mp to her. She holds the mp tightly, taking his pistol away. Misfit aims and fire the pistol at the lights in the control room. She shoots out the lights before the unit of mps and their captain can take action. With the control room lights out, misfit goes into ass kicking mode. Misfit uses all her street fighting, combat training and martial art skills. She knot down, knot out and bring down some of the mps in the dark control room. The mp captain and some of the mps try looking for Misfit. Misfit hit's the mp she is holding on the back of the head. The mp falls unconscious to the dark control room floor. Misfit makes her way to another part of the control room door. The door leads to another stairway out of the jail house. She carefully rushs down the stairway and run out of the jail house. The emergency lights in and around the jail house control room come on. Some of the mps find themselves handcuffed to their desk. The mp captain notices one of the mps do not have a uniform on. Misfit walks away from the military jail house, dress as an mp. The mp captain sees his mps are unconscious in the stairways. He gets on the jail house emergency phone. Mp Captain: "This is a emergency announcement to all military personnel. "One of the prisoner has escape." The emergency alarms sound go around the whole island's military base. Mp Captain: "I repeat, a prisoner has escape." She goes by the rank and name, Lieutenant Timeworth." "She is arrned, extremely dangerous and wearing a mp uniform." "If you see Lieutenant Timeworth, please contact the military police department." "Do not attempt to catch Lieutenant Timeworth." Timeworth is a latin female, six, one, a hundred and fourty five pounds, repeat, Timeworth is extremely dangerous." The alarms continue to go on around the whole island. Mps run down, up, cross inside and outside the base. Units of mps rush out of the jail house and onto the island's fortress/base.

platoons of mps rush out of the jail house and look for Misfit. The mps use the search towers looking for Misfit, but do not find her. Misfit makes her escape somewhere on the base. She is far enough from the military jail house. Misfit goes to see if she can find her teammates. She can not walk around the base freely knowing the mps are looking for her. She is now a wanted woman and not a hero anymore. As long as she is a wanted woman, she must stay out of sight and out of mind. Misfit also hears the announcement going around the base. Mp Captain's voice from the loud speaks on the base, "Lieutenant Timeworth is dress as a mp." Misfit no long care about the rules or military orders. She watchs out for Colonel Bender and any unit of mps. Misfit: "Fuck orders." Misfit keeps walking under the cover of walls, cars and other building on base. Misfit spots karene coming from the Colonel's office.

She comes out from hiding. She grabs Karene and puts her hand over Karene's mouth. Misfit drags Karene into the back of one of the buildings. Karene trys to yell, but Misfit keeps her hand held tightly around Karene's mouth. Misfit: "Relax,... relax, I said relax." "Am not going to hurt you." "Relax ok, don't scream or tum around." Misfit lefts Karene go. Karene, still shaken up by the sudden attack and nervously turns around to see Misfit. Karene does not scream for help. She discover it's only Misfit. Karene sees Misfit is in a military police uniform. Misfit speaks quietly to Karene in the back of the building. Karene: "So, you escape from the jail house." Misfit: "Yeaaaa, well, what does it look like." Karene: "ok,...sweet, but stupid, ma'am." Misfit: "What, your not happy to see me." Karene: "If the Colonel or any mps see you, you will never make it out of jail." Misfit: "Ok, listen karene, calm it down a little." Karene: "Yes,...yes ma'am" Misfit: "Not so loud." "I need a favor." Karene: "Sure, yes ma'am." Misfit: "I need to get out of this uniform and quick." Karene: "Ok ma'am, let me see what I can do." Misfit: "Alright, so everything is cool with us." Karene: "I guest so." Misfit: "Listen Karene, I need to know I can trust you." Misfit looks at Karene with a uncertain expression on her face. Misfit: "Can I trust you, Staff Sergeant Stinson." Karene: "Yes ma'am." "You can trust me." Misfit: "We are cool on this plan." Karene: "Yes ma'am." "Tough girl." Misfit: "Thanks." "I always knew you were a good person." Karene: "You actually escape from the jail house." Misfit moves her head up and down, answering Karene. Misfit: "Yea, like Houdini" Karene: "Yes ma'am, sweet." Misfit: "Stop calling me ma'am." Karene: "Yes ma'am,..sorry." Misfit: "Call me what you just call me." Karene: "You got it." "Tough girl." Misfit: "Right, yes that right, you got it Karene, so, how are you." Karene: "Fine, ok i guest." "How are you doing, Timeworth, since the incident and all."

Misfit: "Well, lets see." "I was doing fine, of couse I got harass after almost getting killed." "Beat up on by Colonel Bender and his gang of mp attack dogs." "Now, I am a escape criminal on the run from the military,...as you can see Karene." "I am fine." Karene: "I see the mp's uniform fits you really nice,..oh wow you're a warrant officer. "Misfit:" Yea, didn't have time to check." Karene: "Yes, I can see that." Misfit: "Thanks, really gald you like the uniform." Karene: "Hey, no problem." Misfit: "So, when can I get some new clothes." "Sister." Karene: "Give me some time and I will have them for you soon." Misfit: "Yes right, make it soon and fast." Karene: "Quick, you better hide, some one is coming." Misfit prepares for a fight. Karene tells Misfit to follow her to a hiding spot in the next building. The spot is so well hiden, that the mps do not see them on their search. Misfit: "Wow, who would have ever known, you smart, clever woman." The units of mps pass right by them. Misfit: "Thanks Karene for sticking your neck out for me." Karene: "Your wellcome, it's not a problem for you." Misfit follows Karene through a secret passage way under the building. Misfit and Karene come out through the other side of the building. Misfit follows Karene into a parking lot full with cars. They get into one of the cars and Karene drives Misfit out of the base.

Misfit stays hiding inside Karene's car, until they get to Karene's little house outside of the fortress. The little house is located far on the island. No one will find Misfit for a long time. Karene: "Let me make a call." Misfit: "Make a call to who, Karene." Karene: "Relax, I am making a call to Peal and the others. Misfit looks around Karene's house. Karene: "Relax tough girl, make yourself at home." "My house is your house." Misfit: "What about those clothes Karene." Karene: "Oh yea, 1 almost forgot." Karene tells and shows Misfit where she can find something eles to where. Karene: "The clothes closet is over there." "Pick out what you want." Misfit goes to the clothes closet and open the closet. She sees Karene like to wear tight clothes. Misfit:" You sexy thing." Misfit picks out a outfit from the closet and changes her clothes. Karene make a few call to others. Misfit goes to sit down in the living room. Misfit looks arounds the living room. Karene: "She here guys,...sitting in my living room." Karene continue to talk on the phone to Peal and the other teammates. Karene: "Yes, she looks ok, from what I can see,..see you guys then." Karene hangs up the phone. Misfit ask Karene if she can take a shower. Karene tells Misfit, "yes." Misfit goes into the bathroom and takes a shower. Karene goes to the kitchen to make two drinks for her and Misfit. Misfit takes her shower and Karene checks outside her house windows.

She is looking for any signs of mps or trouble. Misfit finish her shower and comes out of the bathroom. Misfit: "Is something wrong Karene." Karene: "No, everything looks fine." Karene moves from the windows and hands Misfit a drink of alcohol. Misfit: "Thanks,..um, good,...nice place Karene." Karene:" Yea, thanks, it's small, but dam comfortable." Misfit: "Thanks for the drink, I was thirsty." Karene: "You want something to eat." Misfit: "Yea, I am hungry." "Thanks again Karene." Karene: "No problem." Misfit goes to look out Karene's house windows for trouble. Meanwhile, Karene goes into the kitchen to make some food for herself and Misfit. Karene yells from inside the kitchen to Misfit. Karene: "Would you like a beer." Misfit, still looking outside the living room windows for any signs of trouble. Misfit: "Too tight,..much to fancy for me." Misfit talking to herself. Misfit: "What did you say." Karene: "I ask you, if you wanted a beer." Misfit: "Yes, I would." Karene brings the beer out of the kitchen. She gives one of the beer to Misfit. Misfit: "Thanks Karene." Karene: "Your wellcome tough girl." Here to breaking out of prison." Karene smiles at her friend and her hero. Meanwhile, at the base. The Colonel speaks to the mp Captain over the phone. Colonel Bender: "Find that bitch." "I want her found now," right now." "Eles, I will have your fucking heads." Mp Captain: "Yes sir, Colonel sir." Colonel Bender: "Captain, you and your people better find

Timeworth and her friends quickly." Colonel Bender hangs up the phone on the Mp Captain. Back at Karene's house. All of Misfit's teammates meet and welcome her back, except for Lady Commando, who is not present. Misfit gives her teammates a great big hug.

They all hug her back with a great big hug. Back in the Colonel's officer. The Colonel meets with the Mp Captain, Captain Frank Manena and a unit of mp. A unit of mp bring Lady Commando in for interrogation. Mp Captain Frank Manena interrogate Lady Commando in the island's military police station. Meanwhile, at Karene's house. Misfit and her teammates are so happy to see each other. Misfit's teammates give her a salute. She gives them a salute back. Misfit: "Good to see you guys." Misfit's teammates Peal, Scorpion, Deadcold and Captain Stanly reply: "Gald to have you back,..how did you escape from the jail house,...never through we would see you again,... good to have you back Captain Timeworth,...Misfit." Misfit: "Thanks,...where's Lady." Misfit looks around Karene's living room for LadyCommando. Captain Stanly, Peal, Deadcold and Scorpion reply: "We don't know,?...we thought she was already here."

"She didn't leave with us,..we haven't seen her since she toll us she had to go back to her barracks." Peal: "Yea, didn't see her since she left, right after the big mess-up." "She say she had to go back to her barracks for training and testing." "She said she would meet up with us here." "I throught she would be here already." Karene: "No, you guys were the first to show up." Misfit: "Somethings wrong,..that's not like her." Deadcold: "You know, she still might be in training camp." "Don't worry momie, she will show up." Deadcold reassure his girl friend Misfit, that Lady Commando will show up. Deadcold: "After all, this is a military training camp in a hidden island." "We are away from the world." Scorpion: "Yeaaaa, we are on a hidden island." "Part military fortress, part training and testing base." "Out in the middle of no where." Captain Stanly: "Yes, remember, she just got here for training and testing." Karene: "Yes,..just like the rest of us." Misfit: "Oh, you guys I hope so, if not,..we are already sitting ducks." Meanwhile, in the military police station. Colonel Bender, the Mp Captain, Frank Manena and a unit of mps question Lady Commando. At Karene's house, Misfit and her teammates figure out a plan to save Lady Commando if she in trouble. Deadcold: "So, if she doesn't show up." "She might be capture." "What's the plan, fearless leader." Misfit: "It's time to pay the Colonel a visit, enough bullshit." Peal looks at Misfit with a worry look on her face. Peal: "Then what, the Colonel controls this whole freaking island.' He's going to be ready for us and its going to be hard to get Lady Commando out." "God only knows where they are keeping her. Captain Stanly: "I agree, especially now, the Colonel is going to be looking for trouble." Scorpion: "Yea, by this time the base will be crawling with mps." "We will be walking right into a trap. Deadcold looks at Misfit. Deadcold: "That's right,..but that's not going to stop you." "Right my tough sexy angel." Misfit shakes her head from left to right. She gives the body sign to her boyfriend Deadcold, "no, that won't stop me." Misfit looks at the time and still no Lady Commando. Misfit: "Ha, ha, ha, ha (laughs), right." Deadcold: "After we do this, we gota find a way off this island." Captain Stanly: "First, we have to get our hands on some heavy duty weapon."

"Second, we have to find rides to get us in and out of the fortress, plus the base and third." "We have to find a water vehicle or plane that will hold all of us." Misfit: "I broke out the jail house, so, how hard can it be to rescue Lady and get off the island." Captain Stanly: "Oh, it's going to be very hard, extreme difficult." Peal: "yep, not easy at all." Misfit: "Ok, here's the plan." Misfit and her teammates talk about a plan. Misfit and her teammates are not aware that Lady Commando has been captured by the Colonel.

Colonel Bender uses Lady Commando as bate to set his trap for Misfit and her teammates. The Colonel hooks up Lady Commando to a recording device system. The phone rings at Karene's house. Karene picks up the phone and answer her phone. Karene: "Hello, Sergeant Stinson speaking." On the other side of the phone, a familiar voice speaks. Lady Commando: "Hi, it's me Karene." Karene: "Yes ma'am, How are you doing." Lady Commando: "Fine, listen, I just came out of training and testing, where is your house located." Misfit and her teammates stand inchs from Karene. Karene: "Hold on ma'am." Karene puts her right hand over the mouth piece of the phone. She turns to Misfit and the others. Karene: "She want's to know where my house is." Misfit gives body signals to Karene, telling her it's ok for Lady to come over. Karene: "Do you think that's a good idea." Misfit shakes her head up and down. She gives Karene the body signs for yes again. Karene takes her right hand off the mouth piece of the phone and speaks. Karene: "Hi ma'am, are you still there." Lady Commando: "Yes sergeant." Karene: "Do you have a pen and paper ma'am." Lady Commando: "Yes." Karene tells Lady Commando where her house is located. Karene gives Lady Commando the address and directions to her house. Misfit and her teammates feel their actions might bring their end. Colonel Bender and two platoons of mps head to Karene's house by trucks, cars and by motorcycle. In one of the truck next to the Colonel, sits Lady Commando. Colonel Bender: "Let's go get that bitch." Lady Commando: "Excuse me sir." "She is not a bitch, wait,..how do you know if she is there." Colonel Bender: "You will address me as Colonel sir." "Understand Lieutenant Headman." "I am not one of homies from the hood." Lady Commando: "Yes sir, Colonel sir." Colonel Bender: "Lieutenant Timeworth better be there, got me lieutenant." Lady Commando: "Yes sir, Colonel sir." Colonel Bender: "She's there, you better hope so, young lady, for your sake." Lady Commando: "Yes sir, Colonel sir." Colonel Bender, Lady Commando and the two platoons of mps come with in a mile away from Karene's house. They stop on a sandy beach road. Colonel Bender stops the vehicles of two platoons of mps, before they reach Karene's house. Colonel Bender tells Lady Commando to get out of the truck. He tells her to get into one of the cars. Some of the mps give Lady Commando a empty civilian car. Lady Commando gets into the car and drives to Karene's house. A civilian car shows up at the front of Karene's house. Lady Commando beeps the car horn and stops the car by Karene's house. She is arrive two and an half hours late.

Karene lets Lady Commando into her house. Karene: "Welcome, Lieutenant Headman." Lady Commando walks inside Karene's house. Lady Commando: "Nice place, Sergeant Stinson." Karene: "Thanks ma'am." Lady Commando: "Just call me Lady." Karene: "Alright, look's like everyone's here." Karene and Lady Commando go into the livingroom. They are greeted by Peal, Scorpion, Deadcold and Captain Stanly. Lady Commando salutes her new teammates and they salute her back. Lady Commando: "Nice to see you ma'am." "Nice to see you sir, nice to see you ma'am, nice to see you sir,.where's tough girl." Peal: "Who." Lady Commando: "Tough girl, Misfit, Captain Timeworth." "I know she's here." "I already heard the news, remember I was right there went Karene called, besides, it's all over the base." Misfit comes out of hiding from one of the rooms in Karene's house. Misfit: "Here l am Lady." Lady Commando salutes Misfit and Misfit salutes Lady Commando. They race to hug each other. Misfit: "Good to see you lady." Lady Commando: "You too, tough girl." Misfit: "You don't have to salute me or call me ma'am." Lady Commando: "Ok, if you say so." Misfit: "You guys,..yes I was beat up." "Demote back to lieutenant, now that I am a escaped prisoner of war." "My rank is probably going to be a private again." Misfit's teammates start to laugh. Misfit: "We have a plan to make the Colonel pay." Misfit laughs as she said this to the others. At that monument, unaware to Misfit and her teammates. Lady Commando has recorded every word Misfit and the others have said. The Colonel listen in, and tells the Captain of the military police. Colonel Bender speaks to the mp captain. The Colonel uses the walkie-talkie radio inside the truck. Colonel Bender: "Get your mps ready to move in and capture Misfit and the rest them, move now, quickly Captain." "Make sure you capture Misfit and everyone in that house." "Understand me Captain." Meanwhile, a few feet away from Karene' house, Mp Captain Frank Manena and the two platoons of mps move in on Karene's house. Mp Captain Frank Manena: "Yes sir Colonel." Mp Captain Frank Manena gives the order to the lieutenant of the mp units. Lead by their lieutenant, the units of mps move in to capture Misfit and the others. One hour passes. Everyone in Karene's house is getting ready for pay back on Colonel Bender. They prepare themselves for a trap set by the Colonel. Lady Commando sits in the living room with the others. She looks at Misfit and tells her something the others do not hear. Lady Commando: "Misfit." "Misfit looks at Lady Commando with a distrusting expression on her face. Misfit: "Yea, what's up." Lady Commando: "Sorry tough girl." Misfit: "Lady,..you never call me that." "You ratted on me." "You dirty fucking bitch, you betrayed me." Lady Commando: "Iam so sorry tough girl." Misfit: "And you have the balls to show up here." "I should have known you would be the one to set me up."

Peal: "I don't belive you brought them here." 'You are wired."
Scorpion points his rifle at Lady Commando's head. Scorpion:
"You rat bitch." Deadcold: "We gota get out of here." Misfit,
Peal, Karene, Deadcold and Scorpion rush to the back door of
Karene's house. Captain Stanly: "Go, go." "Come on, let's."
Misfit quickly puts Lady Commando in a choke hold. She
holds a pistol to Lady Commando's left side of her head. Misfit:
"Move." Suddenly, Misfit and her teammates hear vehicles
outside Karene's house. Misfit holding Lady Commando by the
neck and points a pistol at her head. Misfit: "I won't forget this."
"You sold us out and for what." Captain Stanly: "No time for
that." "Let's keep moving, we have to get the hell out of this
house." Lady Commando placed in a choke hold my Misfit, is
forced to move quickly to the back door of Karene's house. She
is very frighten and starts to crys. Lady Commando: "You,..
should kill me,..yes, go ahead,...I sold you out." Misfit: "Dam
fucking A right,.keep moving." Lady Commando: "I, didn't
have any choice." Misfit: "What ever, move." Misfit speaks to
her other teammates. Misfit: "Let's get out of here, there's no
time for this bullshit." Karene leads the other teammates to a
way out. Karene: "Come on follow me." Deadcold: "Move,
move faster, they are inside the house." Peal: "Shit, time to
go fight." The Colonel and the platoon of mps break down
the front door of Karene's house. While, other part of the

platoon of mps make their way to the back of Karene's house, outside. Colonel Bender and the small army of mps races to catch up with Misfit, and her teammates. Colonel Bender and the mps quickly and savagely search Karene's house for Misfit, and the others. Colonel Bender: "Find them, they can't be gone, no." Karene, fortunately has a secret escape route. Misfit and the others make their escape out of the house and outside. Misfit and her teammates hide into the island scenery. Misfit takes her right arm off of Lady Commando. She tosses Lady Commando down on the sandy, planted, beach ground. She bends down over Lady Commando. Misfit holds her pistol to Lady Commando's face. She pulls back the hammer of the pistol. Misfit: "You bitch, any last words, because I don't feel sorry for you, hell, I don't know if I can even feel anything for you." Lady Commando laids helplessly pin-down by Misfit's neels on her arms. Lady Commando: "Shot me." "1 know you want to kill me, sorry, oh god, I don't want to die. Lady Commando still crys. Misfit: "Shut up and keep your voice down." "Die in silence, coward." "You wanted to die before, oh now, you don't want to die." Lady Commando: "Ahhhh, (crying)....I am dead,..she's going to kill me."

Misfit: "One more time." "Keep quite fool, I am about to put a bullet in your head." "Come on, come on take it like a woman." Peal, Deadcold, Captain Stanly, Scorpion and Karene look on in horror, as Misfit is about to kill her best friend Lady Commando. Misfit: "Time to die." Misfit holds the pistol and aims it at Lady Commando's head. Lady Commando silently pray to god, while she looks down the barrel of Misfit's pistol. Peal: "Stop, there must be another way." Misfit pulls the trigger to the pistol. The pistol goes off, but does not fire a bullet. Misfit gets up off the extremely shaken, sweaty, nervous, frighten, crying Lady Commando. Misfit: "This time the gun was empty, the next time you betray me, well,..get up Lady." "You guys help her up,...don't just stand there." Lady Commando laids in a tiny pool of sweat and urine. Karene and Peal give Lady Commando a helping hand from the ground. Misfit looks at Lady Commando. Misfit: "I might think about killing you later." "You better keep moving. Karene leads Misfit and the other team members to a hidding spot. A desert training camp once use by the island's military to train soldiers for combat survival. If the Colonel and the platoon of mps show up earler, or minutes before at Karene's house, Misfit and her teammates would have been capture. Colonel Bender and the two platoons of mps continue to look for Misfit, and the others. Colonel Bender: "Where is she." "Dam, that fucking bitch."

Misfit and the others sit down on the camp ground. They talk about Lady Commando helping Colonel Bender to set them up. Escaping from the Colonel is only one of Misfit's problems. Can she ever trust Lady Commando, ever again. Misfit is not certain she can trust anyone now. Captain Stanly: "I guest they make too much noise." Deadcold: "Good thing we hear them coming." Scorpion: "That's good for us, bad for them." Scorpion and Deadcold laugh with each other. Peal and Karene look through the camp for anything to use for an ambush. Meanwhile, back at Karene's house. Colonel Bender is very anger his plan has failed. He sees the recording device has been left behind on the living room table. Colonel Bender: "Enough of this bullshit." "Find where they went." Scorpion: "Did you see how fast she ran through that small back door." (referring to Misfit) Deadcold: "That wasn't a door." "It was some type of small opening in the house." Misfit: "Lady, get your ass over here." "Front and center." Lady Commando goes to Misfit. She stands in front of Misfit. Lady Commando: "Yes." Misfit hit's Lady Commando with a swift, powerful punch to the face. She knots Lady Commando out cold and onto the ground. Misfit: "I feel a little better now."

Misfit goes to sit down on a bullet box. She thinks of what to do next. At Karene's house. Colonel Bender: "Everyone out." "They can't be far,..I will have them all arrested for helping that criminal." Colonel Bender and the two platoons of mps exit Karene's house. Colonel Bender: "Burn the house down." The two platoons of mps reply: "Yes Colonel sir." Colonel Bender goes to the transport truck. He gets a call on the truck's radio-walkie-talkie. Colonel Bender: "Yes captain." Mp Captain Frank Manena: "No luck finding the prisoner, Colonel sir." Colonel Bender:"No just a burning pile rubbish, we are returning back to base." Mp Captain Frank Manena: "Yes sir, Colonel sir." Colonel Bender hangs up the radio-walkie-talkie and the Mp Captain Frank Manena meets Colonel Bender. Colonel Bender: "Let's go." Colonel Bender climbs into the transport truck and closes the truck's right door. The corporal/driver turn the truck key and the transport truck moves through the island's sandy beach roads. The convoy of mps vehicles follow the Colonel's truck back to base. Colonel Bender sends units of mps to search for Misfit and her teammates. The Colonel and the two platoons of mps go back into the fortress. Colonel Bender talks to the Mp Captain in the military police station. Colonel Bender: "Don't let them get off this island, that's an order captain." Mp Captain Frank Manena: "Yes sir, Colonel sir." Mps, mp's trucks, cars and aircraft search for Misfit and her teammates. Karene leads Misfit and her other team members to other hiding spot in the camp. They go where no one will find them. Karene takes them into a under ground camp with in the camp. Karene makes sure she and the others cover up their trail. Meanwhile, back at what uses to be Karene's house. Eight mps stand guard around the burned area where Karene's house was. The three mps's vehicle sit in front of Karene's house. Misfit and her team of outlaw soldiers wait at the desert under ground camp, until the eight mps are given orders to clear out and return back to base. Misfit and her teammates come out of hiding, when they discover the mps have left. Misfit and her teammates find their way back to Karene's house. Karene: "I hope I don't have to do much cleaning up." Karene goes closer to what is left of her house. Suddenly, a unit of mps come driving up the sandy beach road leading to Karene's house. They spot Karene, but do not see Misfit and the others. The unit of mps come out of their vehicles. The unit of MPS: "Stop, or we will shoot." As the unit of mps approach Karene to arrest her. Misfit and the other members of her team come out.

They tackle the unit of mps and take them out using their combat skills. At the base, the Colonel leaves the military police station. He goes into the transport truck and tells the corporal/driver, "Let's go back to the office." corporal." Corporal/Driver: "Yes sir, Colonel sir." The corporal/driver drives the truck away from the military police station and heads to the Colonel's office. The corporal/driver arrives at Colonel Bender's office. The Colonel gets out of the parked truck and goes to his office. The phone rings in the Colonel's office. He rushs to pick up the phone and answers it. He gets a call from the Alumnus. Colonel Bender and Alumnus spent a hour and a half talking about Misfit. Alumnus: "The plans and the mission must go through without trouble, this has to be done." "Understand Colonel." Colonel Bender: "I under, wait." Alumnus: "What's happenlng." "Colonel." Suddenly, a mp patrol truck pulls up to the Colonel's office. The four mps standing guard in front of Colonel Bender's office, watch the truck stop. They pull out their weapons and go to investigate the mp patrol truck. Misfit and her teammates go into action before the four mps can react. They push the doors of the truck out, hitting the four mps. The four mps try to aim and shoot, but they are knot off balance. A few blows, kicks, punchs, blocks, hurt and put the mps laying on the ground. Misfit opens the sun root to the truck. She fire shots from a rifle above the four dazed mps. The four mps drop their weapons onto the ground. Peal, Karene, Captain Stanly, Scorpion, Deadcold and Lady Commando take the four mps hostage. Alumnus: "Colonel Bender, are those gun shots." Colonel Bender: "No ma'am," no sir, no really ma'am, no, it's not sir." Misfit and her outlaw team of soldiers take the four mps into the building where the Colonel's office locate. The Colonel is suddenly cut short. He stops talking. Misfit breaks down Colonel Bender's office door. Colonel Bender: "Shit, oh fuck no." The group of Alumnus at the other end of the phone reply: "What the hell is going on." Colonel, what's happen." Colonel Bender and the Alumnus hang up the phones. Colonel Bender: "Why you, fucking crazy bitch, your dead. The Colonel pulls out his pistol. He fire at Misfit and her teammates. Misfit uses one of the mps as a shield. She fire her rifle at Colonel Bender. Colonel Bender's bullets hit and kill the mp. Misfit is safe and un-touched by the Colonel's bullets. She fire four more bullets at Colonel Bender. One bullet misses the Colonel, going into his office chair. The other bullets hit the Colonel in the right and left arm. Misfit has manage to injure Colonel Bender in both of his arms. Colonel Bender screams out in great pain. He moves painfully side to side in his office chair. Colonel Bender: "Please don't kill me." "I didn't create this mess, uh. Talking in great pain, Colonel Bender goams in pain. Misfit: "It look's like you created your own mess, sir." "You fucking sneak little bitch-ass punk." Colonel Bender: "Wait,...if you kill me,...you will never leave this island." Misfit: "Yea, so what." Deadcold: "No tough girl,..let me kill that asshole."

Colonel Bender screams out for his very life. He is so frighten by the surprise attack, that he urinate on hisself. Misfit: "No, his ass is my's,..Colonel, are you listing to me." Colonel Bender: "Yes." The Colonel crys in pain. Misfit: "Here's the deal." Misfit tells the Colonel, she won't kill him, on one condition, one large condition. Misfit: "I see you are still hurting, don't worry, your sorry little ass will live." Colonel Bender: "Oh god." Misfit: "Little boy, you wanted to kill me, then,..ok, I see things have gone the other way." Deadcold: "Relax Colonel sir." "We will not kill you today, if everything goes ok." Deadcold picks up the dead mp's body. They face his dead body against the office wall. Scorpion: "We should have killed the Colonel." Colonel Bender: "Oh god, no." Misfit: "No dude, remember we make a deal." "We are trained killers,..but not murderers." Captain Stanly: "Stop your crying Colonel." "Remember to follow orders, sir." Colonel Bender: "Don't kill me, please,..I will follow your orders, anything." "Please, don't kill me." "Ms. Timeworth. Misfit: "Good." Scorpion and Deadcold stand next to Colonel Bender. Deadcold: "Don't mess up sir." Colonel Bender stops crying. He adjust himself before the army of mps rush into the base's headquarters. Misfit looks at the Colonel. She looks at Deadcold and Scorpion. Misfit: "Ready guys." Misfit still holding the rifle on Colonel Bender. Peal, Lady Commando and Karene look at Misfit. Karene: "I think you might want to loss the gun." "Tough girl." Misfit: "I don't know if I want to." "Remember Colonel, I will kill your ass, so don't be a fool." "Understand sir." The Colonel shakes his head up and down. Misfit: "Karene,..thanks. Karene gives Misfit the thumbs up. Deadcold gives Colonel Bender back his pistol. As part of Misfit's plan, the Colonel holds onto his pistol. Deadcold: "We should put our weapons down." Peal: "Yes, good idea." Misfit and her teammates put their weapons down. They can hear the army of mps coming. Military police Captain Frank Manena and units of mps rush into the office, with weapons drawn-out. They point and aim their weapons at Misfit, and her comrades. Mp Captain Frank: "Drop your weapons." Uriits of mps: "Drop the weapons, drop them now. "Mp Captain Frank: "Drop them, now, now, drop, get on your neels, on your neels, you fucking shitheads." The Mp Captain Frank Manena, puts Misfit and her teammates on their neels, hard. Misfit looks at Colonel Bender with a, "you better not fuck us over," look. Units of mps: "Hands in the air." "Let's see those hands, hands where we can see them, now, now motherfuckers, now."

Deadcold: "Guys,..we already put our weapons down and our hands are up in the air." One of the mps snap Deadcold in the face. Mp:" Shut up, stop trying to be a wise guy." Deadcold takes a look at The mp. He looks at him, with the look of a cold blooded killer. The Colonel puts his pistol on the office table. Colonel Bender: "Stop Captain." Mp Captain Frank: "Sir, but, what." Colonel Bender: "You hear me, stop, don't arrest them." Mp Captain Frank: "But sir, she try to kill you." Colonel Bender: "Yes, this was clearly my mistake." Mp Captain Frank: "Sir you told us to." Colonel Bender: "Yes, I know what I told you,..now un-hand them, now Captain." Mp Captain Frank: "Yes sir, but, what about the others." Colonel Bender: "The others too." Mp Captain Frank: "Yes sir, Colonel sir." Colonel Bender: "Now leave my office, Good,..I am still in charge." Mp Captain Frank Manena looks on in complete udder confusion and total anger. Mp Captain Frank: "Let's go people, move it." The Captain of the units of mps and the units of mps leave the Colonel's headquarters. The Mp Captain Frank and the units of mps also take all of Misfit's, and her teammates's weapons. Colonel Bender: "Well, it's done,..you can all go back to your barracks." Misfit: "So,..that's it,...just like that, uhh." Colonel Bender: "Yes,..just like that." Misfit: "What ever." Colonel Bender: "See all of you bright and early for tomorrow mission." Misfit and her teammates look at Colonel Bender with confused faces. Misfit: "Did you say, get ready for the mission." Peal, Scorpion, Deadcold, Captain Stanly, Lady Commando and Karene reply: "Ok." Misfit: "Yea, ok." "Colonel." Colonel Bender:"Ok, ok,..ok what." Misfit, Peal, Scorpion, Deadcold, Captain Stanly, Lady Commando and Karene reply: "Yes sir, Colonel sir." Colonel Bender: "Ok now, get out of my office, except for Karene. Misfit: "We all leave Colonel, sir." Karene: "It's ok tough giri, I will be alright." Misfit and her teammates leave the Colonel's office. Colonel Bender gives Karene some paper work to do. Peal: "It looks like we are the right guys for the mission." "Now this call's for a celebration." Misfit grabs a hold of Deadcold. She hugs and kisses him on the mouth. Misfit: "I think we will celebrate by ourselves." Peal: "You guys, it's still morning, I think we should wait for Karene, we can celebrate in front of the Colonel's headquarters." Misfit and her teammates walk a block away from the Colonel's headquarters. Peal, Captain Stanly, Scorpion and Lady Commando go back to the Colonel's headquarters. They wait for Karene. Peal: "If the Colonel desides to do something foolish to Karene, we will go kick his ass." Misfit and Deadcold go back to Deadcold's place to make love. Misfit and Deadcold make strong passionate love in Deadcold's bed.

Misfit: "You know this might be the last time we see each other." Deadcold: "Maybe." Misfit: "Do you real love me Nick." Deadcold: "Listen, let's make a deal, if we make it back alive, without getting our heads blown off." Misfit: "Yea." Deadcold: "Then, you will know for sure." Misfit: "Then ok, let's do the wild thing until the moming." Deadcold: "You're my type of soldier. "My pleasure ma'am," (Kissing). Misfit: "Your my type of hero." "My pleasure sir, (Kissing). Deadcold: "Yessss." Misfit and Deadcold continue to make love. Moming time has come and the base's 6 am alarms sound through out the island. Colonel Bender's voice can be hear on the loud speaker. Colonel Bender: "All battalions, platoons and units, report to your commanding officers." "ASP." Colonel Bender: "The mission is on." "It's time to do what you have been trained for, kicking ass, so get your gear on and your ass moving." "That's an order." The alarms, phones, knots on the barrack doors and signals, happen every where. Soldiers from all over the island, report to the war/combat headquarters. Misfit: "Time to go to war,..let's have some fun." Deadcold: "I am gald someone is in a good move." Misfit: "Ready." Misfit and Deadcold gear up. They come out of Deadcold's place and head to the war/combat headquarters. Soldiers get their orders and battle plans for the mission are given to high ranking officers. A army of b-52 Hercules planes get gear up. They move and transport soldiers, vehicles, equipment, weapons and supplies into the planes's large cargo area. The Colonel speaks on the phone to the Alumnus, while in the large transport truck. He heads to one of the airfields on the island. Colonel Bender tells the Alumnus about the sneak attack on the island and in the ocean. He tells them about the battle plans to retaliate against the organization of drug carters. Colonel Bender: "Right, yes, I have everything under control now,..yes ma'am, yes, I am sure sir,..right on schedule." Misfit and her teammates, along with several other platoons team up with to form a battalion. The large military transport vehicles are loaded up with thousands of soldiers and weapons. Misfit and her teammates get into one of the large military transport vehicles. The vehicles travel to all parts of the island. Dropping off soldiers and going back to pick up more soldiers going to the airfields. The high ranking officers arrive at the island's airfield. Colonel Bender gives orders to the commanding officers to move their soldiers, weapons, tanks, smaller military vehicles, equipment and supplies into the army of massive b-52 planes.

The commanding officers tell Misfit, her teammates and the other soldiers, "it's time to get some pay back for our fallen comrades." "Let's kick some ass." As Misfit, her teammates and the regiment of soldiers board the planes, soldiers yell out mighty battle cries. Misfit listen, but at the same time she goes back into her memories. She remember when she was only a little girl. Seeing her parents and older brother killed by a jealous, murderous, vicious drug cartel and madman, named Proclus. Back then, Proclus was just a small time drug dealer, who was selling drugs on the street conners for Hostos. Pruclus would also love having sex with many of women, including one married woman. Unfortunately, the married woman tum out to be Misfit's mother. Mrs. Ann Lisa.Timeworth, she and Proclus were long time lovers. Mrs. Timeworth keep her affair a secret from her loving, innocent husband and children. Misfit can remember the killing, if though it happen yesterday. She remembers the foster homes, the foster parents, the street gangs she was in, getting into fights on the streets and at schooi. Memories of the old neighborhoods. People and places flash through Misfit's mind. The court houses, police officers, foster parents, teachers, truant officers, neighbors judges. They were all so tried of seeing Misfit. One day a judge toll her in court, "you can go to jail for 15 years or go to the U.S navy for 15 years." "Make something out of your life." Misfit stands before the judge, jury and court officers. Judge: "Or go to jail, get killed by another jail bird, and, if your lucky, be someone's bitch." "Hey, you might even get hit the jackpot, say, life in jail without parole." "The death penalty." Misfit nervously looks at the judge in her high chair. Judge: "It's your choice young lady. Misfit's choice was the U.S navy. A military life, like her foster mother. Mary Rollen, U.S navy staff sergeant and navy recruiter. Suddenly, Misfit's memories fade into the darkness of her mind. Colonel Bender: "Everyone of you prepare yourselves, this is going to be a hard, very long fight." "Some of you won't make it back,..but give them hell." Colonel Bender looks at Misfit. He walks over to Misfit and stops in front of her. Colonel Bender: "Do you think you will be one of the lucky ones." Misfit: "You should ask yourself that." "Colonel sir." The look from the Colonel's face becomes frighten and worried. Colonel Bender laughs at Misfit's response. Colonel Bender stops laughing. He takes a deep breath. Colonel Bender: "Just joking,.oh, by the way, you are now a second lieutenant, that's, not a joke." Colonel Bender is stiil a little nervous and shaken. Colonel Bender smiles some what nervously at Misfit. Misfit looks at Colonel Bender like a crazed mental patient. Colonel Bender: "Get ready girl." "Those animals are ready for a good fight."

The Colonel backs away from Misfit. Colonel Bender: "Mistit, what a name." As Colonel Bender turns around, Misfit respond before he can walk away. Misfit: "I always knew you were a great big asshole." "Colonel sir." Colonel Bender: "Yes, ha, ha, (laughing), Misfit." "You're a big problem,..but, you will be a greater problem for the drug cartels." Misfit: "Good,..sir." Misfit smiles back at Colonel Bender. Colonel Bender: "You crazy, homicidal bitch." The Colonel walks away. He goes to the front of the plane. Misfit looks at Scorpion, she give's him the thumbs up. He give's her the thumbs up back. Misfit blink's her right eye at Scorpion. The b-52 planes take off into the morning air. They head towards panama. The pilots talk to Colonel Bender and the other commanding officers. Hero Pilots: "We will be reaching the area of attack, in 4 minute, prepare for hostiles." Colonel Bender and the other commanding officers tell their soldiers, "it's time to use your parachutes." "Time to jump." Misfit, her teammates and the regiment of hero soldiers prepare to jump out of the massive b-52 planes. Misfit quickly stands up from the plane's chair. She stands behind other soldier in line ready for the parachute jump. She finds herself at the plane's cargo area ready to jump into bright, blue skies. Misfit: "Excuse me dudes, is this flight going to paradise." The courageously, fearless Misfit jumps out of the b-52 plane backward. Soldiers, still inside the plane, see

Misfit jump from the plane without fear or nervousness. The soldiers yell out of the plane to Misfit, "good luck tough girl, give them hell." Misfit speaking silently to herself." "Yea,.let's give all those bitchs hell." Colonel Bender: "That right Misfit, give them shitheads hell." Colonel Bender speaks silently to himself. Colonel Bender: "Please let someone kill that crazy motherfucker." Misfit rolls over in mid-air, until her body faces the clouds and earth. Peal, Scorpion, Lady Commando and several other battalion of hero soldiers, parachute jump from the b-52 planes. Hero soldiers continuously parachute jump out of the planes and onto the ground below. Only Colonel Bender, some of the high ranking officers and plane's military staff are left on board. The bright, blue skies become full with hero soldiers, small and large military vehicles, equipment, weapons and tanks. Colonel Bender speaks to some of the high ranking officers on the plane. Colonel Bender: "I uses to think I was the crazy, tough sum of a bitch here." "Guest I am not." Colonel Bender turns his head towards the cockpit of the plane. His eyes quickly look through the cockpit windows. Colonel Bender: "Good luck tough girl." The b-52 plane's large cargo doors closes. Misfit hit's the ground, cutting herself loss of the parachute.

She tells herself, to remember what she had been trained for. Soon, other hero soldiers drop from the skies and onto the ground. They also tell themselves the same thing, "remember your training." The rest of the regiment drops from the sky to join Misfit, her teammates and the other hero soldiers. All the commanders of the battalions, give orders to the hero soldiers from the planes. Commanders: "Prepare to engage the enemy." Colonel Bender in the plane, once again speaks silently to himself. Colonel Bender: "I hope, Misfit, the others, take out those drug dealing piece of shit and kill the rest of those fucking animals." Commanders: "Let's kill em all and find that drug lord." The large military transport trucks, other military vehicles, attack helicopters and amphibious military vehicles, are send into battle. Misfit, her teammates and the other hero soldiers are told to, "continue to engaged the enemy." Misfit gear up with her high-tech all weather military camouflage and head phone walkie-talkie. Misfit, her teammates and the other hero soldiers, speak low into their head phone walkie-talkie. Misfit: "Roger that,..with pleasure,.time for some pay back,.. girls and boys." Captain Scorpion. Scorpion: "Tough girl,..time to hit these motherfuckers back. Misfit: "Copy Captain Halls, let's send them to hell." Misfit, Peal, Scorpion, Lady Commando join the battle along side Captain Stanly and Deadcold They and the squadron of hero pilots gives air cover to the ground soldiers on the ground below. Captain Stanly and Deadcold fly their attack helicopter through the bullets, missiles, smoked, fire, skies. Misfit, her teammates and the other army of commando soldiers, become engage in a full heavy frontal assault on the enormous drug cartel's palace. Misfit, her teammates and other hero soldiers go through the battle full streets, unitil they arrive at the palace. They are quickly met with major resistance from mercenary forces protecting the palace. The drug cartels have armed and protected themselves well. Using heavily armed soldiers for hire. Fast, relentless, vicious and powerfull, hardcore action comes from both armies. Large gangs of mercenary trained enemy soldiers and elite commando trained hero soldiers, are injured and killed. The soldiers fight each other hand to hand combat. Every type of weapon created is used by both sides. Misfit, Peal, Scorpion, Lady Commando, Deadcold, Captain Stanly and a regiment of elite commando soldiers, fight and do battle from outside and inside the palace. Misfit, her teammates and the other elite commando hero soldiers, continue to battle through a regiment of murderous, mercenary, enemy soldiers. As Misfit, her teammates and the other hero soldiers come closer to the palace's entrance, they cover more ground. The two sides start to suffer many loss. The Captains give the lieutenants the orders to keep pushing forward.

The lieutenant in charge of the platoon in which Msifit is in, gives Misfit and the other hero soldiers orders to, "push back." "Keep fighting, kill, kill, kill, kill." The enemy soldiers still put up a good hard fight. All lieutenants in charge of the platoons of hero soldiers, give the orders, to continue to push back. Kill and capture the regiment of enemy soldiers. Every hero soldiers orders are the same. Push back, kill and capture the enemy soldiers. All battalions of commando hero soldiers from the island/base, continuously and relentlessly keep fighting. Soldiers on both side continue to die. Soldiers lay injured in the streets and in front of the palace. More violence and vicious non-stop fighting, continues in the drug cartel's palace. Misfit fights, kills and injures any enemy soldier that get's in her way. Misfit: "Move." "Move it, move it,..go, go,..come on move." Misfit continues to lay down some heavy fire power, as she protects her fellow soldiers and herself. Misfit and her comrades cross into the small, narrow street of the drug cartel's palace. Some hero soldiers break through the blockades and gates set by enemy soldiers. Both hero soldiers and drug mercenary soldiers fight even harder inside the palace. Even more soldiers continue to die on both side. Misfit does her best to keep herself alive. What the drug cartel's soldiers lack in years of combat skills or intelligences, they make up in massive numbers of soldiers. Colonel Bender and the other high ranking officers deploy more soldiers. The number of hero soldiers do not match the number of large battalions of drug mercenary soldiers. Misfit, fortunately is not a stupid woman. Misfit tells the low ranking hero soldiers to follow her orders in battle. Misfit speaks silently into her walkie-talkie-headphones. Misfit: "Laid low and keep firing at the enemy position." Misfit radios into Colonel Bender. Misfit: "Colonel sir." "We could use some major fire power down here,..like now." Colonel Bender tells some of the pilots to tell the gunners in the planes, to laid down some fire power opon the drug cartel's battalions of mercenary soldiers. The b-52 planes fire down at the enemy mercenary soldiers. Misfit, her teammates and the other commando hero soldiers, continue to fire opon some of the surprise and fleeing enemy soldiers. A sea of bullets rain down on the massive deployment of drug cartel's soldiers, tanks and other enemy vehicles. Hero tanks continue to pound the mercenary enemy soldiers. Hero helicopters, other hero aircraft and hero vehicles, continue to pound enemy soldiers inside the palace. Soon enemy soldiers are join by more tanks, enemy vehicles and aircraft. Misfit speaks to the other hero soldiers, through her radio-walkie-talkie-headphones. Misfit: "Laid down that smoke screen, now."

The hero forces laid down some heavy smoke concision bombs and grenades. The smoke and the explosions create a smokey, fire full grave, that turns into a blinking wall of heavy, black clouds. The drug cartel's soldiers can no longer see their targets. Misfit, Pea, Scorpion and the other hero commando forces, rush in on the mercenary enemy forces. They kill many of the enemy soldiers. Destroying enemy equipment and vehicles outside and inside the palace. Misfit, her teammates and the armies of hero commando soldiers, battle their way through the drug cartel's palace and into the courtyards, swimming pools and torture areas. Many of the gorgeous women prostitutes, palace's servants and enemy soldiers are killed, injured, or escape from the massive and brutal battle. Misfit keeps her eyes on the enemy soldiers that use the prostitutes and palace's servants as human shields. Some of the hero soldiers kill and injure the prostitutes and palace's servants at the palace's area. No place is safe outside or inside the palace's walls. Misfit, Peal, Scorpion along with a fair amount of hero soldiers, continue to fight their way to a large jail house, used for torture. Misfit uses her fire arms, her martial art, combat skills and other small weapons to kill enemy soldiers, guarding the palace's jail house. Misfit, her teammates and the other hero soldiers kill more enemy soldiers, deep inside the drug cartel's palace. Lady Commando leads another platoon of hero commando soldiers into the palace. Misfit,

Peal, Scorpion and many other hero soldiers clear out most of the enemy for lady Commando and her platoon of fellow soldiers. Lady Commando: "Come in Timeworth, copy, come in Timeworth." Misfit: "Copy that ma'am." Gald to see you make it." Lady Commando:"It's good to hear you are still alive, tough girl." Misfit: "Roger that, lieutenant Headman." "See you at the end of this molherfucker,.Lady." Lady Commando becomes a little teary eye emotional. Lady Commando: "Copy that second lieutenant." Misfit: "Roger." "The ladies of war go back to fighting." Colonel Bender and the other high ranking commanding officers keep radio communications open between them and the soldiers. Misfit and the other hero soldiers. Misfit, her teammates and the army of hero commando soldiers reach the main corridors. The enormous corridors hides small pockets of mercenary enemy soldiers. Misfit, Peal, Scorpion are join by Lady Commando and thousands of hero commando soldiers. They storm the first sets of corridors before they are toll where to find the drug cartel named Top Heavy. Misfit, her teammates and their fellow soldiers follow orders. Taking precaution as they silenlly and quickly move opon the drug cartel, Top Heavy and what is left of his army. They find and kill the hidden pockets of enemy soldiers. Killing enemy soldiers from one corridor to the next. leaving only a small resistance of enemy soldiers standing. The small number of enemy soldiers continue to fight and defend the drug carter, Top Heavy.

Misfit, Peal, Lady Commando, Scorpion, Deadcold, Captain
Stanly, and platoons of hero soldiers make their way to the large,
four, front doors of the main part of the palace. Here, they hope
to find Top Heavy. Our heros, Misfit, Peal, Scorpion, Lady
Commando and platoons of their felow soldiers stand at the
four doors to the main part of the palace. Misfit tells the other
to stay down and keep watch for enemy soldiers. Misfit speaks
to her teammates and to her fellow soldiers. Misfit: "everyone
be quiet, prepare to strike silently and quickly." Misfit looks at
the four doors leading to the main part of the palace. She goes
closer to the four doors and knots on one of the four doors.
Misfit: "Hello, anyone home, comalo ests." Suddenly, bullet
holes flash through the four doors. Misfit jumps out of the way
of the four doors. Bullets come through the four doors. She
moves quickly with the speed of a cat. Misfit ducks down, as she
continues to move away from the damage double doors. Misfit,
her teammates and their fellow soldiers, stay down on the floor.
They are forced to move back from the four, large, damage
doors, to avoid beening hit by the shower of bullet. Misfit:
"So much for a warm welcome." Peal: "Alright, they mean
business." Lady Commandos: "So do we." The bullets continue
to fly through the four, large, damage doors. Misfit, PeaL, Lady
Commando, Scorpion and the platoons of hero commando
soldiers, fire back at the other side of the four, large, damage

doors. Misfit sees the bullets have stop coming from the other side of the four, large, damage doors. Misfit: "Iam going in, cover me." Peal tells Lady Commando, Lady Commando tells Scorpion and Scorpion tells his fellow soldiers to cover Misfit. Misfit gets up from her ducking position and quickly runs to the four, large, damage doors. Misfit can hear the enemy soldiers on the other side, reloading their weapons. Misfit sticks her m16, under toe, grenade launch rifle through a large bullet hole in one of the four, large, damage doors. She fire her weapon into the large bullet hole. Misfit stands back a little She fire a grenade into the bullet, damage doors. Misfit can now see through one of the four, large, damage doors. Mifit: "Peep of boob." Misfit fire more bullets at the injured enemy soldiers from the other side of the door. Peal, Lady Commando, Scorpion and platoons of hero soldiers, fire more bullets through the four, large, bullet damage doors. Misfit, her teammates and the platoons of hero soldiers, continue to fire at the four, large, damage doors. On the other side of the four, large, damage doors, some of the enemy soldiers, are injured and killed. Misfit, her teammates and the forces of hero commando soldiers, fire bullet after bullet through the four, large, damage door. Continuously killing enemy forces inside the main part of the palace.

70

Misfit become hard target to shoot at. Peal, Lady Commando, Scorpion and the platoons of hero commando soldiers, fire opon the left over enemy soldiers. Misfit quickly changes weapons. She take out her rifle, size, gatling gun and aims it straight at the four, large, damage doors. Round after round of small rocket size bullets, tear the four, large, damage doors down to the floor. Misfit then takes out her m16 rile with the under toe grenade launch. She launchs four grenade straight into the main part of the palace. The grenade blow up every living person and thing in the main part of the palace. Piece of the four, large, damage doors fall to the palace's floor. Smoke, fue, blood, body parts, piece of the palace walls, door frames, glass and other debris lay on the palace's floors. Misfit, her teammates and platoons of hero soldiers have a unclear view of where Top Heavy or any surviving enemy soldiers are. Misfit and her comrades move slowly through the main part of the palace. Using precaution and deadly accuracy, Misfit and her cornrades kill off the rest of the surviving enemy Misfit: "'Where is that bastard,..where the fuck,..is he." Misfit makes a call to Colonel Bender and the other high ranking commanding officers by her radio-walkie-talkie head set. Colonel Bender: "Roger, Timeworth." "Did you, or any of the others find and destroy the target." Misfit: "No, copy, we did not find or destroy the target, he's,. sir,..I don't think." Colonel Bender: "Copy, Timeworth. "Did you find and kill the subject, Top Heavy." "Well,..did you." Lieutenant Timeworth." Misfit remembers her family was killed by a drug dealer named, Proclus. Colonel Bender: "Timeworth, copy, come in Timeworth." Misfit comes to reality. Misfit: "No." "He's not here, copy, I repeat." "We have not found the subject, Top Heavy." Colonel Bender: "Are you sure," are you." Misfit: "Yes sir." "I am sure Colonel sir." Colonel Bender: "Ok." "Roger that." "Did you and the others kill everyone." Misfit: "Roger, yes, everyone is dead sir." Colonel Bender: "Copy." "I guess they were right about you. Misfit: "right about what, Colonel." Colonel Bender: "Temper, temper now." "I meant the mission." "You are the one for this job, return to the pick up point." Misfit: "I still don't know what you meant by." Colonel Bender: "Return to the extraction point." Misfit: "Got it Colonel,..no, wait,..probably you don't have it, copy sir." Colonel Bender: "No more games, that's an order Timeworth."

71

Misfit: "Yes sir." "Returning to the extraction point." "Roger." Misfit end the radio-walkie-talkie call. Misfit: "Come on people, let's go, move out." Misfit, Peal, Lady Commando, Scorpion and the platoons of commando hero soldiers walk out of the, bloody, bullet shells, debris and bombed out area. They start walking down the hall to the outside of what was the main part of the palace. Misfit, Peal, Lady Commando, Scorpion and platoons of their fellow soldiers, are met with a hale of bullets. Top Heavy and a platoon of his best mercenary enemy soldiers. Misfit, Peal, Lady Commando, Scorpion and the other commando hero soldiers, are surprise by the attack. They manage to fire back, but some of the unexpected commando hero soldiers are killed in the ambush. Misfit and her comrades uses their minds, weapons and skills to kill the platoon of harden mercenary enemy soldiers. Top Heavy manages to escape into his hidden drug lab/command station. He runs down a stairway hidden by a fake hall column. Misfit runs down the stairway after Top Heavy. Top Heavy hides behind some of the drug mules in the drug lab/command station. Misfit slowly and cautiously comes down to the lower part of the stairway. She stops at the end of the stairway. A mist of bullets hit and go through the stairway's walls. One of the bullets hit and goes into Misfit's right leg. Misfit screams out from the pain caused by the bullet in her right Ieg. She falls forward and out of the stairway, landing on her left side. Misfit trys to fire her weapon at Top Heavy, but he uses the drug mules as human shields. Top Heavy: "Ha, ha, ha, ha, got you bitch." Misfit: "Fuck you asshole." "Ahhhh." (She screams in pain). Misfit never drops her weapon. Top Heavy: "Your dead momie." Top Heavy pushs the drug mules to the right and left sides of the drug lab/command station. He aims his weapon at the injured Misfit laying on the floor. Peal, Lady Commando and Scorpion rush down the hidden stairway to help Misfit. Top Heavy takes his eyes and aim off of Misfit. Misfit quickly aims her pistol at Top Heavy. She aims with deadly accuracy, shooting Top Heavy in the head. Misfit blows Top Heavy brain out. Brain matter lands all over the crack, coke cocaine lab table. Top Heavy's body falls backwards onto the table. Peal, Lady Commando, Scorpion and some of their fellow soldiers hear the gun shots. They come out at the end of the stairway, with weapons ready to fire. Misfit: "He's dead." Misfit talks while still in pain. Peal, Lady Commando and Scorpion, come to the aid of the injured Misfit. Peal and Lady Commando tell the platoons of commando hero soldiers to, "look out, cover us and wait at the top of the stairway." Misfit: "I, could use a little help." "Guys." Her teammates pick her up and take her upstairs. Misfit tells her fellow soldiers to help the drug mules.

72

Misfit: "Ok guys." "You can let me go,.thanks." Misfit radios to Colonel Bender by walkie-talkie headphones. Misfit: "Roger, Colonel." "Come in sir." Colonel Bender: "Yes Timeworth, copy." Misfit: "Yes sir, we found,..the target, the target is destroy,...he's dead." Colonel Bender: "Copy that." "Was going to ask you, if he was still alive, I guest not,..return to the extraction point,..with the target's head." "Copy." Misfit: "Yes sir." Lady Commando: "Want me to do it." Peal: I can do it. Scorpion: I got this. Misfit: "it's ok,..I will do the honors. Misfit hops down the hidden stairway. She cuts the head off of Top Heavy's dead body. Misfit takes the head and places it in a medical bio plastic bag. Misfit, Peal, Lady Commando, Scorpion, the platoons of injured and not injured commando hero soldiers, walk out to the court houses. Lady Commando turns her head towards Misfit. Lady Commando: "Michelle, tough girl." Misfit holds on to her pistol. She hops from her injure and walks along with Peal. Peal helps hold her up from falling onto the ground. Misfit and Peal tum their heads towards Lady Commando. Misfit: "Yes ma'am." Lady Commando: "I just wanted to tell." Scorpion walks in front with the other hero soldiers. A enemy soldier laids injured on one of the court house's ground. The injured enemy soldier fire her weapon at Misfit and the other hero soldiers. Misfit, Peal, Scorpion, Lady Commando and some of their fellow soldiers, quickly move out of the line of fire. Lady Commando along with some of her fellow soldiers, are hit by some of the bullets, from the enemy soldier rifle. Lady Commando is hit in the back, both legs, her left arm and gazed in the neck. Misfit fire her pistol at the injured enemy soldier. She kills the female enemy soldier with five bullets. Lady Commando drops to the ground. Misfit, Peal, Scorpion and some of their fellow soldiers, fire opon the already dead female enemy soldier's body. Misfit, Peal, Scorpion and some of the hero soldiers, rush to Lady Commando's side. Misfit gets on her neels and holds up lady Commando's head. Peal, Scorpion and the others try to aid, and comfort the dying Lady Commando. Lady Commando desperately gasp for air from the bullet injures. She bleeds out blood from her gazed neck and her other body parts. Misfit: "Dam it, fuck, someone get a fucking medicate." Misfit talking and crying at the same time. She let's out a loud screams and holding onto her fallen comrade. Lady Commando grabs Misfit by the back. Misfit looks down into Lady Commando's watery eyes and bloody mouth. Lady Commando speaks very closely, slowly and silently.

73

Lady Commoando: "I..just,.wanted,..to say,..you are,..a,..true best friend." Lady Commando dies in Misfit's arms. Misfit, Peal, Scorpion, the platoons of hero soldiers, join by Captain Stanly and Deadcold, flying above in the attack helicopter, head for the extraction point. Colonel Bender sees Misfit carrying the dead body of her best friend. Misfit's sister, fellow soldier and military budie, Lady Commando. Misfit, Peal, Scorpion, Captain Stanly, Deadcold and their fellow soldiers capture or destroy, all of Top Heavy's army. Top Heavy's palace of prositites, palace's servants, enemy, prisoners of war and his drug mules, are held at the extraction point, ready to be transported onto the oncoming military planes. Misfit becomes battle harden. Shes even more harden for battle, now, then she was before. Misfit carry her best friend and fellow soldier's dead body. Lady Commando life-less body is shown to Colonel Bender. The other high ranking officers pay their respects to Misfit. Misfit stands in front of Colonel Bender. She looks at Colonel Bender with a depress facial expression. Misfit: "I hate this part of war." Colonel Bender: "There's nothing nice about war." Misfit: "I will always have love for my friend." The planes land a hour earler and prepare for boarding. The battalion of commando hero soldiers, escort the platoon of mercenary enemy soldiers into the planes. Misfit walks to the plane carrying the body of Lady Commando. Captain Stanly, Deadcold and the squadron of hero pilots land their attack helicopters at the extraction point. Peal, Scorpion, Deadcold, Captain Stanly and their fellow soldiers, follow Misfit into the plane. Colonel Bender and others watch on, as Misfit takes her dead comrade into the plane. Colonel Bender: "Just another part of war." Colonel Bender takes a good, long look into the far distance battle field. Colonel Bender: "Ahhh,..I love it." Misfit lays Lady Commando's dead body down on the plane's medical bed. Colonel Bender turns around, only to come faces to faces with Misfit: "Just another bullshit mission." "Uh, Colonel sir." Colonel Bender: "Listen up, ladies, gentlemen, let's pack it in and move em out." The Planes's Captains pilots and crew: "Yes sir, Colonel sir." Colonel Bender, the other high ranking officers, commanders and the rest of the battle harden battalion of commando hero soldiers, go into the large, b-52 miilitary planes. Any surviving tanks, other military vehicles, equipment, injured soldiers and dead commando hero troops, are loaded into the planes. Misfit sits monition less, looking at Lady Commando's dead body. Her best firend lays on the plane's medical bed before her. Colonel Bender talks with some of the high ranking officers and commanders. Deadcold, Peal, Captain Stanly and Scorpion comfort Misfit.

Colonel Bender looks over at the hero combatants and Lady Commando corpse. Colonel Bender: "She will be ok." "She will be just fine, trust me." Peal, Colonel Bender, Captain Stanly Deadcold, and Scorpion turns to look at the corpse of Lady Commando. They all turn and look at Misfit. Misfit's anger appears on every part of her face. Somewhat sad, mindless and lost, but she does not shed a tear. The planes taxis down the runway of Top Heavy's airfield. They take off into the sun down skies. Moving through the air like gigantic eagles going higher into the afternoon skies. The b-52 planes head back to the hidden fortress/base on the island. The planes take a longer time getting back. The planes land down on the island's airfields. Coloncl Bender, Misfit, Peal, Scorpion, Deadcold, Captain Stanly, the high ranking officers, commanders and the rest of what is left of the battalion of commando hero soldiers, come out the back of the planes. They get into the large transport trucks, cars and other military vehicles. Moving down the road, leading to the island's highway. Misfit never knew how extremely large the island was. She looks out the truck's window, at the different directional signs posted on the island's highway. All that didn't matter now to her. Misfit's best friend, hang out budie, fellow soldier and comrade was dead. Misfit had to deal with the facts of life and death. Lady Commando had given her life for the mission. She was not coming back, ever. Misfit ask Colonel Bender for permission to drive one of the military motorcycles back into base. Colonel Bender: "Sure, Timeworth." Misfit: "Thanks Colonel." Deadcold gets up from his seat inside the transport vehicle. He goes and stands betweet the two motorcycles, waiting on Misfit. She finishs talking to Colonel Bender and walks towards the motorcycles. Misfit remember's something she took from Top Heavy's palace. Something very important from his drug lab/command center. Colonel Bender: "Sure, what's this Timeworth." Misfit: "I almost forgot to give you this sir." Colonel Bender takes the documents from Misfit's left hand. Misfit: "We found it in that drug dealer's hidden crack house, under the palace." Colonel Bender: "Good work." "Timeworth." Misfit: "Thanks sir." Colonel Bender: "Listen, don't even think about kill yourself." "Meet me and the others at the mission room, second lieutenant" Misfit: "Yes sir, Colonel." Misfit walks over to Deadcold and kiss him on the lips. She hops onto the motorcycle and starts it up. She looks at Deadcold standing there, in some what of a dazed. Deadcold: "Stop, let me come with you." Misfit: "Sorry baby, please understand." "I need some me time."

75

Deadcold: "I understand,..see you later." Misfit grabs Deadcold by the head with her left hand and kisses him on the lips again. Deadcold grabs Misfit by the head with his right hand. They continue to kiss. Misfit and Deadcold unlock lips. Misfit takes off, moving the motorcycle in and out of the island's highway traffic. She rides the motorcycle like a horse soldier. Misfit moves pass the convey of military transport vehicles, trucks, car and other military vehicles riding on the highway. Misfit thinks about the times she spend with Lady Commando. She rides the motorcycle fast, faster, and faster. Misfit keeps her eyes on the highway, but her mind and memories are on Lady Commando. Misfit exit off the highway using a turn off ramp. She drives the motorcycle into a hidden road, leading her into the fortress. She comes onto another hidden road, leading her onto the base. She drives the motorcycle onto a near by parking space. She breaks down in tears thinking about her. Misfit walks to the mission headquarters. She walks pass a new army of commando hero soldiers. They have passed their training and testing. Misfit, Peal, Scorpion, Deadcold, Captain Stanly, Colonel Bender and the old army of commando hero soldiers, watch the new army of commando hero soldiers go through role call. Lieutenant Mcpeters: "Sergeant." Get these soldiers ready for the mission." Misfit, Peal, Deadcold, Scorpion, Captain Stanly and the old army of commando hero soldiers, follow

Colonel Bender, the commanders and the other high ranking officers into the mission headquarters. More new candidates ride into the base for training and testing. Karene stands at attention by the mission headquarter's double, front doors. She Gives Colonel Bender, the commanders and the other high ranking officers a salute. They salute Karene back and go into the mission headquarter's room. Karene meets and greets her fellow soldiers, and teamamates at the mission headquarter's double front doors. Karene rushs into Scorpion's arms. Karene: "Did you miss me, big boy." Scorpion: "Why of couse." Karene hugs Scorpion. She immediately notice someone is missing. Scorpion sees Karene's happy face changes to a face of sorrow and anger. Scorpion becomes sadden, as he tells Karene the bad news. Scorpion: "Sorry,..she." Misfit goes over to Karene and Scorpion. Misfit: "Lady is." Karene: "She was a good person." "She is somewhere peaceful, now." "God bless her." Misfit: "Right." Deadcold: "The meeting is starting guys." Misfit looks at Peal, Captain Stanly, Karene, Scorpion and Deadcold last. Misfit smiles at her teammates. Her teammate smiles back at her. The six walk into the mission hendquarters. Colonel Bender speaks about the success of the mission. Misfit, her teammates and the other hero soldiers listen to Colonel Bender give a heroic speech from the podium.

76

Colonel Bender: "Everyone, even thou we lost some of our comrades in battle." "The mission was a complete success." Misfit, her teammates, commanders, other high ranking officers and the old army of commando hero soldiers, clap and applaud Colonel Bender. Colonel Bender: "Now, I know we killed the drug cartel, Top Heavy, but we are not done with this war." Misfit looks at Deadcold and she turns her attention to Colonel Bender. Colonel Bender: "No, not by a long shot." "The drug lord known as Hostos, is far out of our reach." Deadcold standing next to Misfit, holding her hand. He is focus on what Colonel Bender is saying about the war. Deadcold: "It doesn't seem to end." Misfit, Peal, Captain Stanly, Scorpion and Karene focus on Deadcold. Colonel Bender: "We have lost many soldiers and friends." there will be more losts" Misfit talking quietly to herself and listen to Colonel Bender speak of more war. Misfit: "Never ending war." Peal: "So,..more fighting, more death,.. love it." Colonel Bender: "We did destroy our target and the first mission is completed." Misfit: "Sir." Colonel Bender: "Yes, second lieutenant Timeworth." Misfit: "If you don't mind me asking." "The first mission is completed." "What does that mean." Colonel Bender: "It mean, we have more missions." Misfit: "What, more training, more testing, more missions, more battles, more deaths." Colonel Bender: "Yes, that's just what it mean, you, the other soldiers, me, we all have many missions." "Until this war is over, the missions will continue." Misfit: "So, there are more of these motherfuckers." Colonel Bender: "Second lieutenant Timeworth." These motherfuckers are all over the planet." "We must find the other drug cartels, before we find the drug lord, Hostos." "Yes there are more, Timeworth." Colonel Bender tells Karene to come up to the front of the mission room. Karene: "Yes sir, Colonel sir." Colonel bender moves to the right side of the mission room and sits down. Karene stands in front of the podium and takes out files. The files contain documents. The same documents Misfit gave Colonel Bender earlier. Karene reads the rest of the drug cartel's names and locations. The names of the drug cartels flow through the room. Karene: "Thank you Colonel sir." "And a big thanks to our brave commanders, leaders and to our brave soldiers." Karene pause. She takes a look at Misfit. Karene: "Oh yes,..thank you second lieutenant Timeworth." Misfit, her teammates, commanders, other high ranking officers and the old army of hero soldiers, reply: "Your welcome Staff Sergeant Stinson." Karene goes back to reading from the documents. Karene: "The drug cartel, Top Heavy, has been terminated." "Here are the names of the other five drug cartels, including their leader. Hostos, Death Hands, Murder White, Toy Mine, and Proclus." A light comes on in Misfit's head.

Misfit: "Excuse me Staff Sergeant." Karene: "They are in." "Yes second lieutenant Timeworth." Misfit: "Did you say one of the drug cartels name was Proclus." Karene looks down at the documents. Karene: "Why yes ma'am." Misfit: "Thank you." Karene: "Your welcome second lieutenant Timeworth." As I was saying, they are in all parts of the world." "We are not aware of their really locations, but through information given to us by capture enemy soldiers, people who worked for Top Heavy." "We soon will have the real locations, of all four drug cartels, including the location of Hostos." Peal focus her attention on Captain Stanly. She turns her attention to Karene. Peal: "Staff Sergeant Stinson, when will we know the true locations of the enemy." Karene: "Well,..according to these documents and the information given to us by the enemy soldiers,..we should know in four months or probably Less." Karene: "Anyone eles before I continue." Everyone in the mission room remains silent. Peal: "Thank you Staff Sergeant Stinson." Karene: "Death Hands, Murder White, Toy Mine, Proclus, and their leader, better know as Hostos are extremely dangerous." "These individual, are not to be taken lightly by anyone." Karene continues to talk to other soldiers. Deadcold talks to his teammates about the next mission. Colonel Bender gets a call from his cell phone. He excuse himself from the meeting. He gets up from the seat and walks to a small office, located in back of the mission room.

Colonel Bender closes the office door. Colonel Bender: "Yes, Bender speaking, who I am speaking to." Ms.Wong: "This is Ms.Wong of the C.I.A." Meanwhile, in the mission room. Deadcold: "More missions tough girl." "You ready." Misfit: "Yes sir." "Looks like more fun, boys and girls." Deadcold: "Guys, ready for war." Misfit looks at Karene reading from the documents. Misfit's eyes zoom in on the documents in Karene's hands. Misfit: "Good." "Really good." "The war has just began." Misfit turns her attention on her teammate. Misfit: "1 love having fun." Misfit smiles at her teammates. Meanwhile, outside of the mission headquarters building. Miles away, a smooth, high-tech, tough, camouflage, one person fighter plane, parks in one of the island's airfield. The pilot of the fighter plane is just as smooth, high-tech and tough as the plane. Lieutenant Shawn Dawn open's the cockpit door to his plane. The camouflage pilot get's up from the plane seat. He steps out and down the ladder to the plane. Other military personnel tend to his plane. Tin Soldier walks away from his plane. He takes out his cell phone to make a call. Captain Stanly get's a call on his cell phone. The cell phone call interrupt him, as he talks to Misfit, Peal, Deadcold, Scorpion and the other hero soldiers. Captain Stanly: "Hello." "Captain Morgan.Stanly speaking." Tin Soldier: "Hello sir." Captain Stanly: "Brother."

THE END...

Printed in the United States
By Bookmasters